Visit with characters inroduced in the acclaimed Desire Trilogy by Joan Hohl!

"You're Scared Witless."

"I am not scared," she denied through gritted teeth.

"Ahh, but you should be."

Leslie's heartbeat went crazy. Flint Falcon's low, sexy voice evoked images so erotic, she had to sit down, or she'd fall down. "Are—are you threatening me?" she asked, knowing the answer, yet perversely needing to hear it.

"Only with pleasure, darling." Flint's soft voice had the impact of a caressing hand. "Only with pleasure."

Leslie closed her eyes as an intense thrill shook her body. The man was a sorcerer, she thought, pulling the receiver away from her ear to stare at it. If merely hearing him call her darling in that dark voice reduced her to quivering willingness, what would making love with him be like? The urgent leap of anticipation Leslie felt answered her silent question....

Dear Reader:

Series and Spin-offs! Connecting characters and intriguing interconnections to make your head whirl.

In Joan Hohl's successful trilogy for Silhouette Desire— *Texas Gold* (7/86), *California Copper* (10/86), *Nevada Silver* (1/87)—Joan created a cast of characters that just wouldn't quit. You figure out how *Lady Ice* (5/87) connects. And in August, "J.B." demanded his own story—*One Tough Hombre*. In *Falcon's Flight*, coming in November, you'll learn *all* about . . .?

Annette Broadrick's *Return to Yesterday* (6/87) introduced Adam St. Clair. This August *Adam's Story* tells about the woman who saves his life—and teaches him a thing or two about love!

The six Branigan brothers appeared in Leslie Davis Guccione's *Bittersweet Harvest* (10/86) and *Still Waters* (5/87). September brings *Something in Common*, where the eldest of the strapping Irishmen finds love in unexpected places.

Midnight Rambler by Linda Barlow is in October—a special Halloween surprise, and totally unconnected to anything.

Keep an eye out for other Silhouette Desire favorites— Diana Palmer, Dixie Browning, Ann Major and Elizabeth Lowell, to name a few. You never know when secondary characters will insist on their own story. . . .

All the best,

Isabel Swift
Senior Editor & Editorial Coordinator
Silhouette Books

JOAN HOHL
Falcon's Flight

Silhouette Desire

Published by Silhouette Books New York

America's Publisher of Contemporary Romance

SILHOUETTE BOOKS
300 East 42nd St., New York, N.Y. 10017

ISBN: 0-373-05390-8

First Silhouette Books printing November 1987

JOAN HOHL,

a Gemini and an inveterate daydreamer, says she always has her head in the clouds. Though she reads eight or nine books a week, she only discovered romances ten years ago. "But as soon as I read one," she confesses, "I was hooked." Now an extremely popular author, she is thrilled to be getting paid for exactly what she loves doing best. Joan Hohl also writes under the pseudonym Amii Lorin.

For my daughter and new son-in-law:
Amy and Clifford Kline
Be happy, kids.

One

The sign swayed precariously in the sharp October wind. The guy wires tautened and the sign stilled, then began ascending again toward its final resting place at the top of the tall building.

Standing on the famous boardwalk, broad back to the cold wind whipping off the Atlantic Ocean, straight black hair flying wildly around his gaunt, hatchet-hewn face, Flint Falcon watched the proceedings through dark, narrowed gray eyes. A gust of wind set the sign dancing. The motion accented the logo of a dark bird, wings spread in flight, soaring into the promise of the endless day on the sign's bright blue background.

The barely discernible movement of thin but perfectly defined male lips formed a smile on Falcon's grimly set mouth. The sight of the swaying sign pleased him. Of course, the bird was a falcon. The flight was of the imagination. The endless blue sky represented the absence of time. In a gambling casino there is no time—except, perhaps, to play.

Releasing his visual lock on the sign now being anchored by the workmen, Falcon slowly lowered his intense gaze, his narrowed eyes searching for flaws in the structure. There were none, as he was well aware.

From a large, square, multistoried base, the tower rose majestically into the mist-shrouded sky, slim, straight, the tallest building to date to etch the skyline of Atlantic City, New Jersey.

The tall, slender edifice did not symbolize indulgence of whim. To Falcon the towering building was a monument to perseverance and sheer hard work—his own. It had been a long haul for him, over paths strewn not with stones and rocks but with boulders. The gleaming, buff-toned tower, standing above its counterparts, represented personal achievement to Falcon. Against seemingly insurmountable odds, Flint Falcon had emerged tall and strong, not only unbroken but unbowed. He had won. The proof of his victory rose in grandeur for all to see.

"That's it, Mr. Falcon." The work-crew foreman hailed Flint from the other side of the boardwalk. "The sign's secure. Falcon's Flight is ready to take off!"

"Thanks, Morrisey." A slashing grin altered the expression on Flint's face, lending animation to the granitelike visage. Raising a hand, he returned the foreman's wave; then he swept his gaze up the tall spire to the sign.

The last of the interior work on the building had been completed earlier that week. For all practical purposes, Flint could have opened for business weeks ago. He had adamantly refused to consider it. There had been a holdup on the sign. Flint chose to wait for it. The sign was important. It was his personal mark on the monument. Business as usual would not commence until the sign was firmly affixed.

Tonight Flint would host a second and final party. Like the one he had held last night, it would be a rather unusual affair. The party was for employees exclusively. Since the hotel-casino employed such a large number of regular full-time people and an almost equal number of part-timers, two separate parties had to be given to accommodate them. In good spirit, the employees feted the night before would now turn around and serve the servers.

Not only did Flint have his priorities straight, he knew exactly how to line up his ducks in a row. The customers were of the utmost importance and were to be catered to to the nth degree—or as far as the law allowed. The question of morality didn't enter into it. Flint left the moral issues to each individual and to the theologians. His own conscience was clear. But, as important as the customers were, Flint also knew that without his employees there would be no business to speak of.

As they had been the previous night, the party arrangements were elaborate and lavish. Also as he had the previous night, Flint planned to make a token appearance, then cut out. Parties, even those thrown by him, were definitely not Flint's style.

His long legs making short work of the distance, Flint strode across the boardwalk and through an open doorway. The wide plate-glass door was held open for him by a uniformed security guard who was well into middle age, though that fact was not revealed by the man's trim, muscular physique or his cool, alert eyes. As were most of the other security people, the guard was a retired law officer, this particular man from the highway patrol of a western state. Flint did not surround himself with inept, untrained security, male or female.

The guard dipped his head respectfully as Flint paused to scrutinize the spotlessly clean silver-and-black decor of the thirty-foot-wide lobby. The room separated the smoked-glass doors along the famous boardwalk from the silvered entrance doors to the spacious casino.

"Sign okay, Mr. Falcon?"

A hint of a smile eased the unrelenting sternness of Flint's lips at the note of concern in the guard's neutral tone. The permanent employees numbered several thousand. Incredibly, most of them were aware of how important the sign was to their employer.

"The sign's in place," Flint replied, grasping the long, smooth silver handle on one of the entrance doors. "Why don't you step outside and have a look at it?" he asked as he swung the heavy door open.

"Will do, sir," the guard responded with a grin. Though he wanted to see the sign, the man wouldn't have left his post in the lobby for a second without Flint's permission.

With a barely discernible nod of his head, Flint entered the hushed interior of the casino, which encompassed nearly forty thousand square feet of floor space. His narrow-eyed gaze missing nothing, Flint strolled along the wide central aisle that ran the length of the huge room from the boardwalk entrance to the corridor that branched off to the hotel's expansive registration lobby, which faced Pacific Avenue, one block off the boardwalk.

Flint's own personal choice of silver and black was carried throughout the casino and hotel lobby, the severity relieved by splashes of brilliant crimson. The colors were reversed in the employees' uniforms; crimson predominated, and the trim was in silver and black. On Flint's instructions, the interior design and decoration of the entire complex was stark in comparison to the opulence of the other hotel casinos that lined the boardwalk. But Falcon's Flight reflected exactly the tone of simple elegance Flint had desired to convey.

Before veering off into the lobby corridor, Flint paused to run a final glance over the large, silent room, savoring the sense of accomplishment that swept through him. Within twenty-four hours the room would undergo a drastic change. The silence would be broken by the muted roar from the collective throats of eager-eyed gamblers, both novice and experienced. Added to the human cacophony would be the rattle of slot machines, the low, clear call to play of dealers and croupiers and the music blaring from the strategically positioned bar-lounges around the perimeter of the casino. The anticipation of activity and of money changing hands on the morrow pleased Flint.

Satisfaction glittering in his eyes, Flint strode to midway along the corridor, then turned right into a shorter hallway that ended in a cul-de-sac and an unmarked door that had no doorknob. Drawing a narrow strip of plastic from his pocket, he inserted it into an equally narrow slit in the doorframe. A series of clicks could be heard in the hushed atmosphere; then the unmarked door slid noiselessly into the wall to reveal a small elevator. Entering the lift, Flint pressed the only unmarked button on the panel, which contained six columns of numerically marked buttons. Flint lifted the receiver of the black phone mounted on the wall as the door slid shut.

"This is Falcon," he said when his secretary responded. "I'll be in my office if you need me."

"Yes, sir." The response was quick, brisk and masculine.

Replacing the receiver, Flint watched the floor numbers scroll up in a tiny window above the door. The conveyance came to a smooth, soundless stop when the letters *PH* flashed behind the small pane. The door slid back, and Flint stepped onto the thick carpet that covered the floor of a wide area in front of the elevator, then continued along another corridor that dead-ended at a large window. There were two doors visible, one near the window at the end of the hallway and one directly opposite the elevator.

Sliding the plastic strip from his pocket once more, Flint crossed to the crimson-painted door opposite the lift. As he slipped the plastic strip into a narrow slot set into the door, his gaze skimmed over the two tall, gleaming black-and-silver glazed vases that flanked it. Making a mental note to congratulate the head of the housekeeping department for a job well done, Flint pushed the door in and entered his private domain.

Comprised of two levels, the enormous apartment contained four bedrooms, each with a private bath, a square, spacious living room with an adjacent powder room, a formal dining room, an intimate dining room, a large eat-in kitchen and Flint's office suite, which contained a full bath and a small dressing room.

Flint smiled sardonically every time he entered the place. Not too many years before, Flint's living quarters had consisted of a jail cell that had not been as roomy as his office bathroom, and he had shared that cell with another man. At the time, Flint had yearned for a place of his own; he hadn't wanted much, just one room entirely his own. The irony of it all amused him.

As usual, Flint paused on the landing as he quietly closed the door. He didn't notice the thicker, more lushly piled carpet under his two-hundred-dollar shoes, or that the carpet continued down the three steps into the austerely decorated, starkly beautiful living room. Flint had been in residence in the apartment for over a month; he had grown used to the black-silver-and-red elegance of the room. But what Flint had not grown used to, what always made him pause, was the spectacular view afforded by the floor-to-ceiling wall of glass opposite the entrance.

From his vantage point on the landing, Flint couldn't see the city streets, the boardwalk or even the expanse of grayish-beige beach. His eyes darkening to near black with a feeling resembling hunger, Flint's gaze drank in the panorama of ocean and sky stretching out in all its grandeur to the horizon.

Freedom. Space. The view offered Flint the two intangibles his soul craved. While serving time in a claustrophobic cell, Flint had vowed he would die before he ever lost his freedom again. Flint had also vowed to create his own space—to create an environment where he could metaphorically spread his wings and soar like the Falcon he had been named for.

Flint had no idea how long he stood absorbing the view, nor did he care. There was work to be done, calls to make, contracts to study. A tiny smile of satisfaction cracked his set expression. The work would be dispatched when *he* decided to do it.

Flint Falcon owned fifty-five percent of the hotel casino, which had cost a total of two hundred and eighty million dollars to build. Flint Flacon took orders from no man.

"You look completely wrung out, Leslie."

Sitting back in the seat, Leslie Fairfield smiled absently at the waiter who had just refilled her coffee cup. As the young man turned away from the table, Leslie turned to the woman seated across the table from her.

"You sound like a mother," Leslie chided her friend in an affectionate tone.

"I *am* a mother," the slightly overweight woman retorted. As she placed her delicate tea cup in the saucer, the rattle of the china betrayed her agitation. "I'm also your best friend, and I'm worried about you." She frowned, the expression forming tiny lines at the corners of her soft brown eyes.

Her own green eyes darkening with emotion, Leslie reached across the table to grasp her friend's hand. "I don't want you to worry about me, Marie. I promise you I'm perfectly all right." A spark of amusement flickered in Leslie's eyes. "You have enough to occupy your time keeping up with that three-year-old dynamo son of yours, not to mention the dynamo's father, without adding me to your list of concerns." The gleam in Leslie's eyes took on a devious glow. "How is Tony Sr., by the way?"

"Tony Sr. is fine." Marie Ferrini frowned her impatience. "And don't change the subject. I *am* concerned about you." Her full lips tightened. "You look beat. You need a break from the pressure."

"I know," Leslie said. She took a sip of the hot coffee in the cup before continuing. "I have four more performances, then I'll be finished with the play."

"You'll be missed," Marie said warmly. "Your reviews have been terrific. 'Not since the magnificent Kathryn has a beautiful redhead so graced the boards,'" Marie said with a flourish, quoting the praise of one usually acerbic critic.

"Umm," Leslie murmured and smiled with satisfaction. "I'm grateful for the good reviews, but I know when it's time to bow out." Her smiled faded. "It's getting stale. I no longer *am* the character, I'm merely *playing* the character."

Marie's nod conveyed understanding; an actress herself, she could easily understand her friend's waning enthusiasm. Leslie had been performing her current role for ten months without missing a single performance. Since the play was about the sympathetic relationship between two women helping each other deal with the devastation of divorce, Leslie was onstage for almost every scene. There was also the added factor of Leslie's emotional involvement with the role, as she had suffered through the same form of devastation as the character she played. Marie silently cursed Leslie's former husband for the damage he had inflicted on the actress.

Consigning Leslie's ex-husband to the hell she believed he richly deserved, Marie smiled brightly. "So, what are your plans?" But before Leslie could answer, she added chidingly, "I hope you're not even thinking about another long-running play!"

Shaking her head, Leslie drew a long cigarette from a gold-toned case and lit it before responding. "No, I'm not." She exhaled sharply, then continued, "I'm thinking about a long-running vacation."

"You need it," Marie observed, frowning as she watched Leslie puffing nervously on the cigarette. Though Leslie's personal experience with divorce had added depth to her portrayal of the demanding role, the cost had been high to her physical and mental health. In Marie's opinion, Leslie was very near the breaking point.

"I know." Leslie crushed out her cigarette, then immediately lit up another. "Although doing the play was exhilarating, it was also exhausting. I'm tired." Her mouth curved in a wry smile. "But I feel restless, unsettled, oddly dissatisfied...." Her voice faded, and she sighed.

Marie gave an echoing sigh. "I'd say it's time you took a vacation. Have you considered a cruise?" she asked.

"No." Leslie grimaced. "While I like looking at the ocean, I have no desire whatever to be either in it or floating on top of it." Her lips smoothed into a smile.

"I will be seeing the ocean, though. I've reserved a room at a casino hotel, and I'll be leaving for Atlantic City the day after my swan-song performance."

"You're going to the seashore in October?"

Marie's incredulous expression drew a soft burst of laughter from Leslie. "My plan is to make a splash at the tables, not in the ocean," she chided.

Marie didn't join in with Leslie's laughter. Her lips turned down in a deepening frown. "Didn't you spend three entire nights gambling in Las Vegas while you were staying with your cousin Logan in Nevada last fall?" she asked suspiciously.

"Yes," Leslie replied calmly. "Why?"

"Well..." Marie drew the word out.

"Well what?" Leslie asked, lighting yet another cigarette.

"And didn't you make several quick trips to Atlantic City since then?" Marie went on doggedly.

Leslie smiled sardonically. "More than several.... So?" she asked, impatiently.

"Sooo." Marie wet her lips, then blurted out, "I just hope this gambling thing isn't becoming compulsive with you."

"Compulsive?" Leslie looked stunned for an instant, then the delightful sound of her husky laughter filled the air. "Oh, Marie!" she gasped. "What would I do without you?"

"I have a sneaky suspicion that you'd manage very well," Marie retorted, flushing with pleasure.

A gentle smile replaced the laughter on Leslie's soft lips. "Dear friend, I assure you that I'm in no danger of becoming a compulsive, wild-eyed gambler." Sobering, she crushed out her cigarette, then swallowed

the last of her now-tepid coffee. "The money I spend
in the casinos means nothing to me—as you know."
Her elegant eyebrows peaked questioningly.

Marie had little choice but to nod. All of Leslie's
friends were aware of her attitude toward money, and
they had all benefited from it in one form or another.
The only value money had for Leslie was the pleasure
she derived from it, whether spending it on herself or
lavishing it on her friends in gifts or outright loans. On
being chastised or teased for her lack of thriftiness and
failure to prepare for the future, Leslie's response was
always the same: *Life is really very short, and there are
no pockets in a shroud.*

Like most humans afraid to face the fact of her own
mortality, Marie despaired of Leslie's attitude and
continued to squirrel away every extra dollar against
the nebulous mirage of tomorrow. And she continued
to frown at Leslie's imprudent life-style.

"Don't glower at me," Leslie pleaded, unsuccessfully hiding a wicked grin. "Will it relieve you to know
that I really haven't gambled away all that much
money?"

Though Marie's expression was blatantly skeptical,
she again nodded her head.

"Well, I haven't," Leslie said with flat emphasis,
her grin fading. "Believe it or not, I win quite often
and break even as often as I lose." She lifted her
shoulders in a careless shrug that caused her glorious
mane of deep red hair to ripple like a living flame. "I'd
judge I've spent about as much as it would cost for a
good analyst—" her soft lips curled cynically "—and
I've had a lot more fun."

"An analyst!" Marie exclaimed, her eyes wide with alarm. "I didn't know you were thinking about consulting an analyst."

"I'm not," Leslie said soothingly.

"But you just said—"

"I said that I derive more enjoyment from time spent in the casinos than I would lying on a couch telling my sad tale of woe to an analyst," Leslie clarified.

Marie sighed. "I simply don't understand you, Les."

"I know." Leslie smiled. "But don't worry about it; I understand me perfectly."

"But are you sure you're not just kidding yourself?" Marie argued. "Don't most addicts claim that they really don't need their fix?"

"Oh, I never said I don't need it," Leslie replied at once. "I do need it, and I know it."

"But—" Marie began.

"But it isn't the gambling I need," Leslie said, interrupting the other woman again. "It's the escape that I need." Her lips tilted up as Marie's curved down in a frown of confusion. "It's the ambience of the casinos, the atmosphere," she explained. "For some inexplicable reason I forget everything else while I'm there, whether I'm actually playing or merely drifting around observing others at play." She laughed softly. "I'm probably not explaining this very well, but while I'm there there is no pressure, no stress, no sense of time either running out or closing in. While there, I feel unencumbered...." She hesitated a moment, then murmured, "Free." Leslie's green eyes glowed as she smiled at Marie. "I have no idea how long it will last, but for now the casinos are my bolt-hole, my hideout. And yes, I do need that escape.''

''And you don't consider it a weakness?'' Marie studied her friend carefully, for the first time noting the taut lines of strain bracketing her fantastic eyes and the vulnerable look about her sculpted lips. She felt a pang when those vulnerable lips parted to release a weary-sounding sigh.

''You'll never know how much I appreciate your concern, Marie,'' Leslie said, her eyes brightening suspiciously. ''But for now, my periodic escapes are the only thing keeping me strong.''

''Then go to it!'' Marie urged intensely. ''And to hell with the cost!''

Leslie's laughter burst around them like a sudden shower of shimmering sunlight. The advice was completely out of character for her frugal friend, and as such it was all the more warming to hear. Grasping her hand again, Leslie smiled directly into Marie's serious brown eyes. ''Thank you, friend,'' she murmured around the thickness closing her throat.

''For what?'' Marie's voice was also husky.

''For your support, even though you're not convinced that I'm doing the right thing.''

Five days later, Leslie tossed her luggage into the midsize car she rarely got the opportunity to drive and paid a small fortune to garage, and put her defensive-driving lessons into practice weaving in and out of the congested Manhattan traffic. Once clear of the city, she loosened her white-knuckled grip on the steering wheel and relaxed to enjoy the relatively short run to Atlantic City.

Since she'd deliberately chosen the off-peak hours to make the trip, traffic was light and moved smoothly on the New Jersey Garden State Parkway, allowing Leslie some leeway to ruminate on the events of the night before.

Surprisingly, since the role she'd been doing for nearly a year had begun to stagnate for her, there had been an electricity to Leslie's final performance that had brought the audience to their feet with a standing ovation for her as the final curtain had been lowered. She had been presented with four bouquets of roses, and numerous single blossoms had been tossed onto the stage at her feet. Laughing, crying, Leslie had taken three curtain calls and had greeted what seemed to her to be a horde of well-wishers in her dressing room afterward.

After the crowd had finally dispersed, she had barely had time to remove her stage makeup and change before being whisked from the theater to a cab and then into the current *in* nightspot, where a party for her had been arranged by the cast and crew of the production company.

Marie and her husband had been waiting there for Leslie's arrival along with most of her other friends. There had been music and an abundance of food, a few more tears and a lot of laughter before the party had wound down in the early hours of the morning. As the group had parted company, there had been reminders called out to Leslie to keep in touch, and there had been warm handshakes and even warmer hugs and again a few more tears. And then Leslie had gone home...alone.

Blinking against a surge of tears, Leslie steered the car onto the off ramp, then onto the Atlantic City Expressway. With her first glimpse of the tall buildings etching the Atlantic City skyline, Leslie recalled the last few moments of the phone conversation she'd had with Marie before leaving, and an impish smile tilted her lips.

"Have fun, but get some rest, too," Marie had admonished her like a mother hen. "I don't want to see a single line of strain on your face when you get back."

"I'll work at it," Leslie had promised. Then, half teasing, half serious, she had added, "Who knows? If I just happen to run into a tall, dark, handsome devil of a man, I just might indulge in a blazing affair."

Leslie was still smiling at the memory of Marie's encouraging laughter as she brought the car to a stop alongside the Valet Parking sign outside the Falcon's Flight hotel.

Two

—

Unaware of the appreciative male glances that skimmed the length of her legs as she stepped from the car, Leslie draped her coat over her shoulders like a cloak, offered the doorman a brilliant smile along with a generous tip, then swept through the entrance and across the lobby as if she owned the hotel. Then, glancing briefly over her shoulder to see if the bell captain was following with her bags, Leslie strode into the broad, rock-hard chest of the man who *did* own the hotel.

Thrown off balance, Leslie whipped her head around as strong hands grasped her upper arms. A startled gasp became lodged deep in her throat as she gazed into the dark, expressionless face of the most intimidating male Leslie had ever had the misfortune to run into—literally or otherwise.

"I, ah, that is, I—" Leslie was very seldom at a loss for words . . . until now. There was something so formidable about this man that she could barely think coherently, let alone translate her jumbled thoughts into decipherable language. Instead of her usual precise speech, what stuttered out of her mouth was a garbled attempt at apology. "I am, ah, I—I'm sorry!"

"I'm sorry to hear that. I'm finding it rather pleasant."

The man's stonelike visage didn't alter by so much as a crack. Not a hint of a smile softened the severity of his thin male lips. There wasn't a shadow of emotion in his shuttered gray eyes to reveal his thoughts. If it hadn't been for the fine thread of sensuality woven through his low tone and the gentle flex of his fingers into her tender flesh, Leslie would have misunderstood his meaning entirely.

But there was that thread of sensuality, and that thread drew the dangling ends of Leslie's frayed thoughts together. As the realization that the upper part of her body was pressed tightly to his hard chest exploded in her mind, tiny flares of response ignited spontaneously throughout her body.

Suddenly feeling overwarm, Leslie blushed, then stiffened. He removed his grip on her upper arms at the same instant she moved to step back. Leslie found her voice in that same instant.

"I beg your pardon," she said, attempting a cool response. "I'm afraid I wasn't watching where I was going." Cringing inwardly at the throaty sound of her normally husky voice, Leslie forced herself to meet his direct stare.

He didn't return her smile. He didn't relinquish her gaze. But his lips did move—fractionally.

"There is no need for an apology." The tone of his voice was now as remote as the expression in his eyes. "I'm afraid I wasn't watching where I was going, either."

As she eased back another step, Leslie narrowed her long, exotic green eyes, intuitively convinced he was lying; instinct assured her that this particular man always watched where he was going. Strangely, as she backed away from him, the combined scent of spicy cologne and pure male overpowered her. Suddenly feeling trapped within the invisible wisps of a fragrance that was uniquely his, Leslie sliced a glance at the busy registration desk

"You're checking in?" he asked without inflec tion, arching one nearly straight black eyebrow.

"Yes." Leslie's voice had roughened to a whisper.

"Allow me." Briefly flicking his hand to indicate that she should follow him, he pivoted and strode to the registration counter, ignoring the restless crowd waiting to check in with an arrogance the most talented dramatic actor would have envied.

Even while she asked herself why she was obeying his dictate, Leslie followed in his wake, coming to an uncertain stop one step behind him. There were three clerks manning the desk, an extremely attractive middle-aged man, a smoothly handsome younger man and a lovely young black woman. Hurried but unharried, the clerks performed their duties with cool efficiency, for the few seconds oblivious of the dark, silent man observing them. Then, as if feeling the intensity of his regard, the young woman glanced up. Her eyelids flickered with recognition an instant before a dazzling white smile brightened and enhanced the beauty of her face.

"Good afternoon, Delhia," he said politely. Then, not waiting for his greeting to be returned, he turned to grasp Leslie's arm, drawing her to his side. "This lady is my guest. If you'll hand me the card to the Spanish suite, please," he continued, "I'll see to the formality of signing in later." Before he had finished speaking, the unsmiling man held out his right hand imperiously.

Startled, confused and becoming distinctly uncomfortable at the frankly curious stares from the people milling in front of the desk, Leslie drew herself up to her full height, preparing to announce to *him* and everybody else that she would wait her turn. The clerk rushed into speech before Leslie could utter a word.

"Certainly, Mr. Falcon," she said crisply, spinning away to carry out his order.

Mr. Falcon. The name reverberated inside Leslie's head. The name of the hotel was *Falcon's Flight*. Leslie swallowed a groan of dismay. She'd careened into the owner of the damned hotel! She was about to attempt another, more comprehensive apology when another thought ricocheted through her mind. The arrogant, imperious Mr. Falcon had informed all and sundry that she was *his* guest, and that *he* would attend to the formality of signing in later! So, then, what did that make *her* look like?

Distracted by her speculations, Leslie was unaware of two computer-coded plastic cards changing hands. Falcon's low, politely toned voice jarred her into awareness.

"If you'll come with me." Stepping out in front of her, Falcon moved directly into the crowd. Understandably, considering his formidable appearance, those who blocked his path shuffled around to allow him passage.

Feeling the speculative appraisal of every person in the lobby forced Leslie to follow him simply to escape the uncomfortable sensation of being weighed and measured for value per pound. Head up, shoulders back, she tossed her flaming mane like a mettlesome filly and strode after the man who moved with the fluid grace of a soaring bird.

At the bank of elevators, Falcon passed by the other hotel guests waiting for the lifts and walked to the very last set of double doors. There was a small sign marked Private in plain block letters on one of the doors. Dipping his fingers into a pocket, he withdrew a narrow strip of plastic. As Leslie came to a stop beside him, he inserted the strip into a slot in the wall. The doors swooshed open. Inclining his head slightly, he ushered her into the conveyance.

By the time the car began to ascend, Leslie was simmering with an explosive mixture of embarrassment, humiliation and anger. She felt like some man's kept woman. She felt like *this* man's kept woman! Leslie didn't like the feeling.

In a silence that seemed to vibrate with mounting tension, the cubicle swiftly rose to the fifteenth floor, then came to a smooth stop. When the doors slid apart, Falcon motioned for her to precede him into the wide carpeted corridor. His hard, expressionless face revealed not a hint of emotion; his unusual eyes betrayed not a shadow of feeling; his lips barely moved as he murmured directions.

"The suite is to your left, the third door along the hallway."

Sweeping by him, her coat flaring around her like a royal mantle, Leslie strode down the corridor, lips compressed to contain the angry words burning her tongue. At the third door she paused, her back ramrod-straight, staring at the words Spanish Suite painted in gold script in the center of the crimson door. The red color sparked her simmering anger into fiery rage. Red, the color associated with . . .

"I hope you'll be comfortable here," Falcon said, pushing the door open and again motioning for her to precede him. His low, polite tone broke her reserve.

Quivering with fury, Leslie took three strides into the room, then spun to face him, chin up, eyes blazing. "You deliberately let me walk into you in the lobby, didn't you?" she said grittily as he shut the door quietly.

"Yes."

The absolute absence of inflection in his low voice sent an apprehensive chill down Leslie's spine. The complete lack of expression on his harshly chiseled face increased the tremors, making her quiver. She was a mature, self-confident woman, Leslie reminded herself. Except for one weak period comprised of a few weeks when she'd been devastated by divorce, she had been taking care of herself for a long time. Surely she was not afraid of this dark, silent man? With a sinking sensation in the pit of her stomach, Leslie acknowledged the fear closing in on her.

"But why?" she demanded, confusion concealing the panic in her voice.

"The obvious reason." Falcon's lips tilted in a mocking smile; the mockery was directed at himself. "You swept into the lobby like a queen," he went on, his voice lowering as he slowly walked toward her. "That fantastic hair swirling around your shoulders, your beautiful face haughty," he continued, coming to a halt mere inches from her. "And in this place I'm the king," Falcon concluded, as if his statement explained everything, which, of course, it did.

King! Leslie fought to control her erratic breathing. More accurately, the man was a devil! She went still as the word settled in her mind, resurrecting the echo of her own flippant remark to Marie.

If I just happen to run into a tall, dark, handsome devil of a man, I just might indulge in a blazing affair.

Well, this man certainly was tall, and he was dark. But handsome? Lowering her lashes over her glittering green eyes, Leslie examined Falcon's chiseled features one by one. His head was well shaped, his ears nicely formed. His wide brow was partially concealed by a swath of thick, silky-looking straight black hair. His nose was a trifle long, but narrow, and there was an almost delicate flare to his nostrils. His cheekbones were exceptionally high, very prominent, and as hard-looking as his jutting, squared jawline. His lips were unrelentingly thin. The dark, slightly coppery skin that covered all was taut, with the gleaming patina of well-cared-for leather.

Yes, Leslie decided, feeling a strange excitement uncurl inside, this man definitely was handsome—in the way some imagined the devil to be handsome. The realization was both alluring and frightening.

"Not exactly the face a well-bred girl takes home for mother's approval, is it?" Falcon observed in a dry tone, revealing emotion for the first time. His tone held a hint of amusement, and it sparked her own.

"A concerned mother would grab her daughter and run screaming for police protection," Leslie retorted, every bit as dryly. His reaction startled and confused her.

Falcon's features locked and a spasm of something resembling bitterness flickered in his eyes. He suddenly looked very, very large and very, very dangerous. Thoroughly intimidated, Leslie eased one foot back slowly, preparing to bolt if he made a move toward her. His sharp eyes noted her move and his features relaxed, really relaxed, relieving the look of strain.

"Don't panic, I'm not going to touch you," he said in a soft, reassuring tone. Then he did something that stopped her breathing entirely: Falcon smiled, and it was like a burst of warm sunlight after a cold rainstorm. "Yet—" he added in a tone so sexy it sent tiny fingers of excitement scurrying madly through her body. "But soon, very soon," he promised. "And you're going to love every minute of it."

Panic sent out conflicting signals that froze Leslie where she stood. *The man was absolutely crazy,* she thought wildly. And so was she— *She believed him!*

Denying a sense of inevitability slowly expanding in her mind, Leslie drew in a calming breath and reminded herself that she was an acclaimed actress. And if ever she had been called upon to play a difficult role,

it was right here and now. She had to act her way out
of this situation, beginning with this damned red suite!
Stepping into the role, she tilted her head regally and
composed her features into a disdainful expression.

"I seriously doubt that," she finally responded in a
scathing tone every one of her previous directors
would have applauded. "I think I'd like to leave now,
if you don't mind," she continued in a commendably
frigid tone. "I'd really prefer another, less crowded,
hotel."

"But I do mind." This time Falcon's smile was slow,
sensuous, nerve-crackling. Leslie was positive she
could hear the little pops at each tiny nerve ending.
"You have absolutely nothing to fear, Miss—?" He
arched an eyebrow, prompting her.

Leslie hesitated, but decided he could probably find
out who she was simply by making a few calls. She
shrugged fatalistically. "Fairfield," she said distinctly. "Leslie Fairfield." Leslie wasn't sure if she felt
insulted or gratified when he failed to recognize her
name. She must have felt insulted, for her husky tone
acquired a decided edge. "Is there anything else you'd
like to know, Mr. Falcon?"

"Everything," he returned softly. "Eventually."
Abruptly but smoothly he turned and walked to the
door, startling her with the silent swiftness of his
movement. "I'll leave you to get settled in," he said,
pulling the door open. "Your luggage will be delivered momentarily. Feel free to call me if the service is
not to your satisfaction."

"Do you happen to have a first name, Mr. Falcon?" Leslie called as he stepped into the corridor.

"Yes, Leslie." He turned to favor her with a brief but flashing smile. "The name's Flint."

"Figures."

Though her tone had been low-pitched, Leslie heard the sound of his soft, appreciative laughter as he gently shut the door, leaving her to her speculative thoughts in the elegantly appointed suite decorated in red, black and silver.

That woman's dangerous.

The thought stopped Flint cold in the act of inserting the plastic strip into its wall slot. Dangerous? To him? A calculating smile flickered over his lips. There wasn't a woman alive...

The elevator doors parted silently, interrupting Flint's thoughts. Stepping into the cubicle, he shot his wrist from his white French cuff and glanced at the round gold watch covering his pulse. Flint noted his increased pulse rate as he noticed the time. The pulse was fast; he was late.

Grimacing, he punched the floor button he wanted and glared at the closing doors. He'd been on his way to a meeting when he'd caught sight of Leslie sweeping into the lobby. Her haughty air and regal carriage had literally stopped him in his tracks; the impact of her lovely, elegantly sculpted features framed by that mass of red hair swirling around her arrogantly squared shoulders had hit him with the force of a body blow.

For an instant that seemed to shimmer through him into infinity, Flint stood transfixed, confused, staring into her face, gripped by a gut-deep yearning for...what? Though slightly pale, her skin was living perfection. Free of artificial color, her lips induced a shivery response within him. Her hair appeared to crackle like a flame, compelling his hands to seek warmth in the silky strands. And her eyes! A silent groan had tightened his throat. Her eyes were the clear green of a summer glade, inviting him to lose himself in the shadowy depths.

That endless instant in time produced the most profound sensation Flint had ever experienced. He had completely forgotten the meeting, the meeting *he* had called. Without hesitation he had moved to intercept Leslie, deliberately allowing her to walk into him. His body still hummed from that brief contact with hers.

The pulse beating beneath the gold watched kicked into high gear. Flint's lips tightened into a grim line. Dammit! He wanted the redheaded witch! He could feel his body growing taut with sensual excitement. His blood was running wild and hot. He wanted, needed—

Flint clenched his long, tapered fingers into his palms until the knuckles glowed whitely through the coppery skin. Control. Control. Flint forced himself to breathe slowly, deeply, while he silently chanted the single word. His objective was reached before the elevator doors glided apart at the conference-room floor.

His thin lips curling into a satisfied smile, Flint stepped out of the elevator and strode along the wide corridor. There wasn't a woman alive capable of capturing *this* Falcon, he assured himself confidently.

The memory of his eyes haunted her.

Leslie shivered. *Flint.* What was it about his eyes? she asked herself, moving restlessly to the window.

Falcon's eyes saw too much while revealing nothing. And the color—what was the color? Leslie frowned. Gray, she decided. Falcon's eyes were gray, dark gray...except at the odd moments when they appeared to be blue or almost black.

Leslie's lips curved into a wry smile. Like the man himself, Falcon's eyes defied definition, at least at this point. Perhaps later, after she knew him better...

The content of her thoughts brought a gasp to Leslie's lips. What was she thinking? She had no intention of getting to know Flint Falcon! The man had the look of a predator. Leslie shivered in reaction to the image of him that rose in her mind. The only problem was that though she tried to convince herself the shiver was caused by his formidable appearance, Leslie was afraid there was more than a hint of sensual excitement woven through her response.

Uneasy with the direction in which her thoughts were drifting, Leslie spun away from the window, determination stiffening her spine. She had to get out, not only of the suggestive suite but of the hotel itself. But first she had to locate her luggage.

Searching for the phone, her eyes narrowed as her glance settled on the red-and-gold instrument placed on a black lacquered table next to a plush velvet sofa. Decadent, she thought, frowning. The suite was blatantly decadent. Her expression disdainful, Leslie strode to the table. She was reaching for the red receiver when a soft tap sounded on the door and a quiet voice penetrated the panel.

"Bellman, ma'am."

"And not a moment too soon," Leslie muttered. Straightening, she turned from the table just as the phone trilled. Dammit! Leslie glanced at the phone, then at the door, then back at the phone as it rang again. Then she sighed in exasperation. "Come in," she called to the bellman. The door opened as she reached for the receiver. "Yes?" she said impatiently into the phone while trying to motion the bellman to wait.

"Have your cases been delivered?"

All rational thought ceased at the soft sound of Falcon's voice. A shiver trickled down Leslie's spine. Although his query was mundane, the tone of his darkly exciting voice seemed to hint at pleasures too exquisite to be mentioned aloud.

"Yes, just now." Leslie was so intent on concealing the tremor in her voice that she didn't hear the door closing behind the bellman.

"Good."

Leslie gripped the receiver. How had he managed to inject such a wealth of sensual meaning into a word as simple as "good"? she asked herself, nervously moistening her suddenly dry lips. A twinge of pain in the fingers clutching the smooth plastic receiver brought her to her senses.

"Mr. Falcon, I—"

"Flint," he interrupted in that disconcertingly soft tone. "Please."

His tone was so very polite. Yet beneath that politeness lurked the sensuous intent Falcon had made no attempt to conceal from her earlier. The shiver at Leslie's spine increased in intensity and spread to tingle the short hairs at her nape. Her heartbeat quickened; her breathing grew shallow. Swallowing convulsively, she opened her mouth to tell him she was leaving the hotel immediately. Falcon spoke before she could form the first word.

"Leslie?" His tone wasn't quite as soft or smooth.

"Yes?" Leslie paused to gather breath and courage. "Flint, I'm leaving—"

Again he cut her off. "Okay. I'll be tied up for most of the afternoon with meetings. Will six-thirty be convenient for dinner?"

Of all the overbearing—Leslie's mind went blank from amazement. His self-assurance was incredible. Anger flared as her senses came together. Did the man actually believe that all he had to do was breathe to command her attention? Worse still, was he convinced he could gobble her up like a tasty tidbit simply by installing her in an opulent suite of rooms? The speculation set fire to Leslie's temper and brought the actress to the fore.

"Have dinner at your own convenience, Mr. Falcon," Leslie said in her best haughty tone. "I won't be here. I'm not leaving to spend the afternoon playing or shopping, as you've obviously assumed. I'm leaving the hotel, period. I'm sure I can get a room at the—" Flint again exercised his infuriating talent for interrupting.

"Why are you running away?" he inquired in that same polite tone. "Are you afraid of me, Leslie?"

No more than I'm afraid of a stalking panther, Leslie thought somewhat wildly. But of course the threat of having every one of her beautifully manicured, fashionably long fingernails clipped wouldn't have forced her to admit to her confusing sense of excited intimidation.

"Afraid? Of you?" Leslie laid the haughtiness on so thickly her tone sounded almost British. "Not likely, Mr. Falcon."

The man laughed. "You're afraid," he chided politely. "Or are you playing a variation on a theme of coyness?"

"Playing coy!" Leslie's tone came to within a hair of being a shout. "I outgrew *coy* at age six!"

"I'm delighted at having my initial impression of you confirmed," Flint murmured. "Now, about dinner—"

"I just told you I won't be here for dinner!" Leslie exclaimed, gratified at the opportunity to interrupt him. "I am leaving this blasted hotel to find a room that doesn't look like a courtesan's salon."

This time Falcon was satisfied with a low chuckle. "The suite does lend itself to the idea of debauchery, doesn't it?" As he didn't expect an answer, Flint didn't wait for one. "I'll have you moved out of there at once," he went on in a brisk tone.

Leslie was beginning to feel as if she was trying to clutch at fog, "Mr. Falcon—Flint—listen very carefully," Leslie said slowly and distinctly. "I do not wish to remain in this hotel. Have I made myself clear now?"

"Sure," he drawled. "You're scared witless."

"I am *not* scared," she denied through gritted teeth.

"Ahh, but darling, you should be."

Leslie's heartbeat went crazy. Falcon's low, sexy voice evoked images so erotic that she had to sit down or fall down. "Are—are you threatening me?" she asked, knowing the answer, yet perversely needing to hear it.

"Only with pleasure, darling." Flint's soft voice had the impact of a caressing hand. "Only with pleasure."

Leslie closed her eyes as an intense thrill shook her body. The man was a sorcerer, she thought, pulling the receiver away from her ear to stare at it. If merely hearing him call her "darling" in that dark voice reduced her to quivering willingness, what would making love with him be like? The urgent leap of anticipation Leslie felt answered her silent question. Suddenly she wanted the pleasure he was threatening her with, wanted it with a shocking intensity. In wavering slow motion, she brought the receiver back to her ear when she heard him call her name.

"Falcon, I..." Unaware that she'd used his surname, Leslie paused to draw a calming breath. Flint used that pause to his advantage.

"I like to hear that, darling." There was a huskiness to his low voice that had a melting effect on Leslie's bones.

Leslie's response was a soft, revealing moan.

"I'll have you moved at once," he said, repeating his promise. Then, with only the briefest of hesitations, he asked, "All right?"

Leslie had difficulty speaking; she usually did when she couldn't breathe. She wanted to argue. She wanted to stand firm in her decision to relocate to another hotel. She wanted to give him a resounding *no*. Instead, she caved in like a warmed marshmallow. "All right."

"And six-thirty for dinner?" Flint insisted, his tone beguiling now.

"Yes." For long moments after he'd hung up, Leslie stared at the receiver she held clutched in her hand, trembling as she faced the extent of her acquiescence. She was not a child, nor was she naive. She knew exactly what she had agreed to, and it involved a lot more than a change of rooms and a meal. For whatever reason, Flint Falcon had singled her out, not only as a dinner companion but as a bed partner as well. *She* was to be the Falcon's dessert. Leslie knew it, and the knowledge was shocking, simply because it was so very exciting.

Leslie had just remembered to replace the red telephone receiver when the same bellman returned to collect her and her luggage. Following the man in the distinctive black-and-silver uniform along the corridor, Leslie frowned when he bypassed the cul-de-sac containing the guest elevators. Hiding her confusion, she sailed along in his wake, silently wondering where the hell he was leading her.

The bellman's destination was a small unmarked elevator at the end of a small hall off the main corridor. Leslie was beginning to get an inkling of what to expect as she stepped into the boxlike lift, and for some reason the plain black phone mounted on the elevator wall reinforced her expectations.

The elevator came to a smooth stop, the doors slid apart noiselessly and Leslie trailed the bellman over plush carpeting to a crimson door flanked by tall black-and-silver vases. After inserting a narrow plastic strip into a slot in the door, he stood back, motioning for her to enter. With increasing but concealed nervousness, Leslie crossed the threshold into the broad foyer of what she was now convinced were Flint Falcon's personal quarters.

"Quarters" was hardly adequate to describe the apartment. Her breath caught on a silent gasp, Leslie gazed at the expanse of windows opposite the entrance. The view of sky and ocean appeared endless, and was exhilarating and intimidating at one and the same time. Not unlike Flint Falcon himself, she mused, as were the sparse but elegant furnishings. Her gaze drifted from the window to briefly skim lacquered tables and lush, expensive upholstery.

"If you'll follow me, please?" the bellman asked, jolting Leslie out of her bemusement. At her cool nod, he crossed the wide landing, descended the three steps to the living room and strode to the wrought-iron-railed curving staircase that led to the second level.

Trailing her fingers along the cool metal rail, Leslie felt her stomach muscles tighten as she mounted the stairs. The room the bellman ushered her into brought a sigh of relief to her dry lips. Though spacious and exquisitely decorated in muted red and antique gold, it was obviously a guest room and not the master suite. Nerves eating at her patience, Leslie duly noted the walk-in closets and lavish connecting bath the bellman dutifully pointed out to her before taking his leave with a smile, a slight bow and a polite refusal of the tip she offered him.

Finally alone, Leslie stood motionless in the center of the room, her bemused gaze slowly moving from the gilt-edged white furniture to the double-size chiffon-draped canopy bed, listening to the echo of her own voice of a few hours earlier as she'd made her flippant statement to Marie.

But tall, dark and handsome or not, was she seriously considering an affair with Flint Falcon? Leslie asked herself, suppressing a tremor of anticipation. The man was dangerous, she reminded herself, a shark who would very likely grin as he took huge bites out of her confidence.

Her imagery sparked a memory of Falcon's flashing white smile, and a delicious shiver jangled Leslie's nerve endings. Flint's sex appeal was potent. Leslie felt the allure of his attraction in the most feminine parts of her body. Her lips burned, her breasts tingled, and she experienced a melting sensation inside.

It was ridiculous and crazy, but Leslie was forced to admit that she wanted Flint Falcon, that instant, no questions asked. Shaken, her body suddenly weak, her breathing shallow, she walked to the end of the chiffon-draped bed and sank gratefully onto the edge of the mattress.

Distracted by her churning thoughts, Leslie stared blankly at the rich warmth of the room. The trappings were unimportant; she didn't see them. Looking inward, she saw a thirty-seven-year-old woman, mature, self-assured, successful in her chosen career and hungry for a man she didn't know, a man she had met less than two hours before. Ridiculous? It was absolutely insane!

It was also absolute fact. And unless he was amusing himself in some sort of game, Flint Falcon was as hungry for her as she was for him.

The consideration brought a frown to Leslie's soft lips. What, she wondered, was the untamed Falcon thinking about at that very moment?

* * *

An emerald surrounded by diamonds. Ice encircling fire. The idea appealed to Falcon's sensual nature and his sense of humor. His decision reached, he acted upon it in his usual swift manner.

"Let's wrap it up quickly, gentlemen." Flint sent a narrowed, nearly black glance skimming over the startled faces of the men seated around the long conference table. Once his course was charted, his plans stated, he expected results. He had little patience for executives unable to keep pace with his thinking, and they all knew it. Flint Falcon hadn't arrived at his present position by being slow and dull-witted—they all knew that as well. "Sum up, please." Falcon leveled his sharp gaze on the sandy-haired man directly to his right.

As Falcon's dapper secretary took down every word with lightning speed, the men around the table briefly and succinctly summarized the situation in their respective areas of expertise concerning the enormous job of operating the hotel and casino. When the man seated on his left finished speaking, Flint nodded and pushed back his chair.

"Congratulations, gentlemen. We are now ready to roll." Standing, Flint again favored each man with a glance. "You've worked well together and have formed a cohesive, formidable team." His thin lips quirked into a smile. "I'm glad you are all a part of Falcon's Flight." The expression on each man's face was a clear indication of how rare, and so how valued, were words of praise given by their employer. "Meeting adjourned." Inclining his head at the table, he turned and strode from the conference room.

A few minutes later, Flint acknowledged a security guard's greeting with another nod of his head and, striding by the door the man held open for him, stepped onto the boardwalk. With a definite destination in mind, Flint moved at a rapid clip, his sharp-eyed gaze sweeping the people strolling the boards, missing nothing, yet appearing to be unaware of anything but his own thoughts.

Unobtrusive, yet every bit as sharp-eyed, two well-dressed men followed at a discreet distance behind Falcon.

Three

———

Leslie stood by the side of the bed, an indecisive frown marring the perfection of her carefully applied makeup. It was 6:05. In the hours since the bellman had relocated her, Leslie had explored the apartment—except for a suite of rooms that was locked— helped herself to a cup of tea in the utilitarian, well-stocked kitchen, unpacked her suitcases, had a long relaxing bath and prepared herself for the evening ahead. Her glorious mane of hair gleamed flame red in the well-lighted, mirrored closet doors. Her slender, taut figure was enhanced by lacy lingerie. Her long, supple legs were encased in hose so sheer they looked bare. The frown line on her brow was caused by her indecision about what to wear.

Hands on her hips, Leslie pondered the two garments spread out on the bed. One of the dresses was a wool blend in a creamy off-white, the other a figure-hugging sheath in a vivid teal blue. Since she hadn't the vaguest idea what Flint's plans for the evening were, choosing one garment over the other was difficult. Raising her right hand, Leslie nibbled on her thumbnail and silently chided herself for making such a big deal out of the whole process.

"Wear the white and spare the manicure."

A surprised gasp burst from Leslie's lips, and she spun around to face the doorway and the man who stood in it. All kinds of funny sensations went skittering through her at the sight of him. Looking every bit as dangerous as she remembered, Flint Falcon was positively devastating in dark evening attire and a glaring white dress shirt with tiny pleats. Rattled, Leslie momentarily forgot that her own body was barely covered in lace.

"You startled me!" she said accusingly, unaware of the allure of her heaving chest. "How did you get in here?" Leslie knew the question was ridiculous the instant she blurted it. Falcon's wry look merely underlined the fact.

"I live here." His lips curved into a sardonic smile. "Or hadn't you figured that out yet?"

"Of course I had." Leslie's insides clenched as he pushed away from the doorframe and sauntered toward her. "I'm not a fool, Mr. Falcon." Hiding her her body's response to him was impossible. Leslie groaned inwardly as his gaze lowered to the hard peaks pushing against her lacy bra.

"I didn't think you were, Miss Fairfield." He slanted a dark eyebrow questioningly. "It is *Miss* Fairfield?"

"Yes, it is Miss Fairfield," Leslie said, trying to keep her tone even. Never before in her life had Leslie experienced such difficulty in simply breathing. The phenomenon infuriated her.

Falcon chuckled. "Wear the white," he repeated, drawing a long black velvet box from his pocket. "And wear these with it." Flipping open the lid, he held the box out to her.

Leslie was not without sophistication, yet the sight of the emeralds and diamonds wrenched a gasp from her throat and widened her eyes. The set consisted of four pieces: a collar necklace, a narrow bracelet and a pair of button earrings, each the size of a quarter. The design was simple and elegant and the stones were brilliant in their perfection. Motionless, Leslie stared at the pieces in stunned bemusement.

"You don't like them?" Falcon asked, his soft tone jarring her into alertness.

"They're beautiful, but—"

"You prefer other stones?"

Leslie shook her head. "No! It's just—"

Falcon again spoke over her hesitant words. "I chose the emeralds because they match your eyes, and the diamonds because they reflected your cold facade."

His phrasing broke the spell of bemusement. "Cold facade?" Unconsciously Leslie drew herself up to her full height. "What do you mean?" Her eyelids narrowed over green eyes that were beginning to glitter as brilliantly as the gems in the velvet box.

Falcon's lips twitched. "The facade you're presenting to me now," he drawled, turning to stroll to the door. "Wear the white, and the baubles, darling." He paused in the doorway to sweep a dark-eyed gaze over her body. "Unless you'd be willing to indulge my desire to see the gems adorning your naked body?"

Leslie was at once incensed and excited. Ignoring his question, she snapped the box closed. "I can't accept them," she said with what she thought was commendable firmness.

Falcon looked unimpressed. "Of course you can." His thin lips curved into a smile of sheer enticement. "Now get dressed, darling, before I decide to give in to a stronger appetite and cancel our dinner reservation." He shut the door on his final word.

The man's absolutely mad! The condemnation joined the mass of conflicting emotions swirling around in Leslie's astounded mind. Did he actually believe— She cut the thought short. Of course he did. And, in all honesty, Flint Falcon had every reason to believe she'd not only accept his gift but earn it as well! She had meekly allowed herself to be ensconced in his apartment. What else was the man to think?

Releasing the catch on the box, Leslie glared at the sparkling gems. The man had taste, she'd give him that. And, really, he couldn't possibly know about her disinterest in jewelry. Smiling, Leslie tossed the box onto the bed. What the hell, she thought, scooping up the white dress. She had committed herself to an affair with Falcon when she'd crossed the threshold into his apartment; she might as well face the fact.

His back to the room, Flint gazed through the window at the expanse of night sky beyond the artificial lighting along the boardwalk. Although his indolent posture gave the impression of ease, inside he was at war with himself. The silent battle raged for and against involvement with Leslie Fairfield.

There was still much to be done in the launching of the hotel-casino; the last thing he needed was to get mixed up with a woman, any woman, but most especially a white woman.

But, that pale-skinned redhead certainly had extracted an instantaneous response from deep within him.

On the other hand, he couldn't afford the time required to conduct an interesting affair.

But considering the woman in question, any amount of time spent, no matter how brief, would be worth the effort, and probably more than merely interesting.

A searing shaft of intense desire put an end to Flint's inner turmoil. The arguments pro and con were academic, anyway. Falcon knew nothing could now make him veer away from the course he'd set. He wanted Leslie Fairfield, wanted to possess her with an intensity that was almost shocking, and he had every intention of doing so.

Leslie's light tread as she descended the curving staircase drew Flint from his introspection. His decision made, he shrugged off considering the possible consequences of his liaison with her. Idly wondering if she had condescended to wear his gift, a dry smile in place in the event she hadn't, Flint turned away from the window.

The view inside the living room was worthy competition to the endless sweep of night sky. His breath catching in his chest, Flint stared in open admiration at the woman standing poised at the foot of the stairs.

The white dress gleamed in stark contrast to her ti-
tian mane, the draped bodice of the garment enhanc-
ing the full curves of her breasts and the skirt swirled
gently around her shapely calves. Her eyes reflected
the glitter sparked off the precious stones by the indi-
rect ceiling lights. But the dress and the jewelry were
only the setting for the magnificence of Leslie, who in
Flint's opinion was the gem without price.

"Lovely." Falcon was unaware of having murmured the compliment aloud, and of the note of near
awe in his low voice. "Absolutely lovely."

"Thank you." Leslie swallowed against a sudden
tightness in her throat. "They are exquisite pieces."

Flint frowned. Then he began walking toward her,
an amused smile tilting his lips. "I meant you," he
said, reaching out to lightly touch the collar circling
her smooth throat. "They are stones, cold and inani-
mate." The tip of his finger slid from the collar to her
silky skin. "The warmth of your flesh gives them fire
and life." His finger drew a feather-light line down the
edge of the dress where it draped the curve of her
breast.

Leslie felt a chain reaction of tiny explosions from
the spot where his fingertip rested to the most secret
reaches of her body. She had been complimented before, touched before, yet never had she felt such an
immediate, urgent response. A cool shiver trickled
down her spine. A breathy sound whispered through
her parted lips.

"Flint, I..." Her voice faded in the heat from his
passion-darkened gaze.

Moving slowly, Flint trailed his finger up to her
neck. He lowered his head as his hand curled around

her nape. Mesmerized, Leslie stared at the miniature reflection of herself in his eyes and parted her lips. From a distance she imagined she heard a low, ravenous growl.

"I'll muss your makeup." His mouth hovered over hers. His breath misted on her trembling lips.

"I don't care." Her voice was faint, reedy, a wisp of sound that went no farther than his mouth.

"I told the maître d' to expect us at six-thirty." He moved his head to brush his lips over hers.

"I don't care." She lifted her head in a fruitless attempt to capture his mouth.

"Later, darling," Flint promised in a sexy, bone-melting tone. "There's an employees' party tonight, and I must put in an appearance." Rueful amusement edged his voice. "And unless I get you out of here within the next few seconds, I'll be tempted to say the hell with dinner, the party and the entire world." Removing his hand from her nape, Flint stepped back. A groan rumbled from deep in his throat when he caught sight of the liquid green fire in her eyes. "Keep looking at me like that and I'll chuck my good intentions to take you to dinner," he warned, taking another step back.

Leslie sighed, then came to her senses. The spell was broken, but the melting heat lingered on to warm her body. "I am hungry," she admitted with a small, self-conscious laugh.

"For me?" He gave her a glimpse of his devil grin.

"Flint!" Leslie wailed in protest.

Moving quickly, he walked over to her again. Bending, he placed his open mouth against the curve of her neck. "I like to hear you call me Falcon." His tongue teased her quivering flesh. "It arouses something atavistic in me." With a final gentle nip with his teeth, he quickly moved away from her. This time he indicated the door with a sweeping motion of his arm. "I'll claim a larger bite later," he murmured, laughing softly as she swept by him regally.

Situated on the third level of the hotel, the restaurant was elegant in decor and lighted by muted chandeliers and by flickering candles placed in the center of each table. The cuisine was French.

Displaying the gallantry and flair of one of the queen's musketeers, the maître d' escorted them to the secluded table kept for Flint's exclusive use. Declining a before-dinner drink, they began the meal with onion soup with bite-size croutons floating beneath a thick cheese topping. From the soup they progressed to the chef's specialty of tender medallions of veal in a burgundy sauce served with tiny browned potatoes and thick spears of white asparagus. Of course, they were treated to the Caesar salad, prepared in grand fashion at their table by the fussy maître d'.

Conversation was limited to generalities throughout the consumption of the meal, which suited Leslie; she used the time to regain her composure. Feeling more in control, she allowed herself to relax over the rich coffee and the fiery liqueur Flint ordered for both of them.

"You mentioned an employees' party?" she probed, raising the small liqueur glass and taking a sip. The liquid ran down her throat with a pleasant burning sensation.

"Yes." Lifting his glass, Flint silently toasted her before tasting the drink. "There are too many of them for a single bash, so I divided them in half. We had the first one last night." The fine wool material of his suit coat moved with the light shrug of his shoulders. "It's my way of welcoming them all as employees of Falcon's Flight."

"It's very considerate of you," Leslie observed, and she meant it.

Flint's smile was dry. "I've been called a lot of things, but considerate is usually not one of them." He tossed off the last of his drink, then set the glass down. "At any rate, they'll earn it." His smile turned sardonic. "Don't make the mistake of casting me in the role of considerate white knight. I assure you I'm not."

Exchanging her glass for her cooling coffee, Leslie cradled the delicate gold-edged cup in her hands, brought it to her lips and stared at him over the rim. Her lips curved into a chiding smile. "Okay. You've told me what you're not; now tell me what you are."

"Tough, ambitious, ruthless and determined to achieve the goals I set for myself," he answered without hesitation.

Though his bluntness chilled her, Leslie maintained her composure. "I understand ambition, I have more than my share myself." She sipped her coffee, savoring the full-bodied taste before continuing. "Perhaps I should have asked you who you are instead of what you are."

Flint glanced at his watch. "We must leave soon," he said. "There's not nearly enough time to swap life histories."

Leslie arched one delicately curved eyebrow. "Would you tell me anything if there were time?" Her skeptical tone indicated her doubt.

"You can always try me sometime when we're alone," he invited softly. Then, insinuatingly: "I fully intend to try you."

"Falcon." Leslie's tones was sharp with warning; her unsteady hand rattled the cup as she placed it in the saucer.

"You know, I get all kinds of wild thoughts and re-actions when you call me that." His soft laughter ne-gating his assertion, he got to his feet and moved to the back of her chair. "Are you ready?" Bending over her solicitously he whispered, "For the party, and what-ever else comes to mind?"

Rising slowly as he eased the chair back, Leslie tilted her head to give him a cool look. "Gambling comes to mind, Mr. Falcon. I came to Atlantic City to play." Head high, she swept from the restaurant, silently congratulating herself on attaining the exit without humiliating herself by tripping over her own strangely unsteady feet. Her feet nearly betrayed her when Flint murmured close to her ear.

"There are games and then there are games, Miss Fairfield." His hand came to rest at the small of her back. "What is your specialty?" Applying a light pressure, he guided her toward the escalator that would take them down to the second level of the ho-tel.

Moving with all the outward appearance of a queen while inwardly trembling like a teenager daring to flirt with an older, more experienced man, Leslie stepped onto the metal stair. Angling her head, she gazed up

at him from wide, innocent, amusement-sparkled
eyes. "Why, I don't have a specialty, Mr. Falcon."
Her dark eyelashes fluttered down, then up again.
"You see, I'm extremely proficient at all the games."
As she turned to step off the moving stairs, his low
chuckle followed her.

"Cagey." His murmur had the impact of a brazen
caress. "And flirtatious. You do realize that you're
playing with fire?" He slanted an eyebrow at her.

Leslie smiled. "I recognize the heat."

White teeth flashing, Falcon laughed aloud. "Believe me, it's going to get a helluva lot hotter before
this night's over."

Leslie stopped walking. Her vision filled by the tall,
dark man, Leslie was unaware and unconcerned with
the shops that lined the broad expanse of floor space
and the hotel guests who strolled the carpet from one
glittering display window to the next.

"I wouldn't make book on that, Mr. Falcon." Her
cool tone gave clear indication that flirtation time was
over. Flint had struck a nerve, and she was retaliat-
ing. "I do not appreciate being taken for granted."
The bracelet circling her slender wrist shot angry-
looking sparks at him as she raised her hand to brush
her fingers over the necklace and one earring. "Please
don't make the mistake of thinking these stones have
bought you a second of my time, in or out of the bedroom." Her smile was chiding and cold. "I command
an excellent salary, and I'm not for sale."

"If I believed you were, I wouldn't be here with you
now." Flint's eyes were as cold as her tone, their color
now almost black. "And I don't appreciate being
taken for a fool, Miss Fairfield." He was also obliv-

ious of the ebb and flow of those passing by. Capturing her hand, he drew it slowly to his hard-looking lips. The mere brush of his mouth over her fingertips induced an alarming weakness in Leslie. Narrow-eyed, Flint observed the tremor that washed over her when he touched the tip of his tongue to her palm. "There's an explosive chemistry at work between us. I know it, and so do you. So let's forget the games." His tongue flicked out again, eliciting a muffled gasp from Leslie. "I want you. I think I've made that obvious. You want me, too... and I know it."

Suddenly hot and cold and much too aware of where she was, Leslie glanced around and murmured a warning. "Falcon! Someone will hear you!"

"Let them." His shrug said a lot about his confidence and arrogance. "I haven't got time to concern myself with what others think. Right now, you're my major concern." A smile touched his lips, a smile so blatantly sexy Leslie felt the effect in every inch of her body. "I enjoy the flirtation, darling—it adds an exciting edge to the anticipation. But I have no patience for the game-playing."

Leslie was breathless and more than a little rattled, yet she'd understood what he'd meant. Flint had said she was his major concern *right now*. And, since absolutely the last thing she was looking for was any kind of permanent relationship, his attitude suited her— didn't it? Made uneasy by her speculative thoughts, Leslie snatched her hand away from his and lifted her chin in challenge.

"I wasn't aware of playing games," she said, "or of trying your patience."

"You're playing a game right now," Flint chided. "I believe it's called dodge 'em." He reached for her hand again and anchored it to his side by twining his fingers with hers. "Flirt, darling, tease, darling, but no shadow-dancing, please, darling," he murmured whimsically. "We're going to have an affair. We both know it." He flashed his devil grin at her. "Hell, it's already started." He stroked the outer edge of her hand with his finger, and his grin spread when she shivered. "Let's dispense with the talk of buying and selling and get on with the more important issue of mutual giving. Agreed?"

Nonplussed, Leslie stared at him as he slowly raised one dark eyebrow questioningly. By using the direct approach, Flint had very neatly maneuvered her into admitting the truth. Though slightly irritated by his method, Leslie couldn't deny a sense of amusement. Subtle Flint Falcon wasn't, but then he wasn't devious, either.

Her expression wry, Leslie did the only thing she could do; she gave him a rueful laugh. "Agreed."

Until he heard Leslie say it, Flint refused to recognize the tightness in his chest and the breath caught in his throat. With a sensation close, too close, to amazement, he allowed the breath to ease silently through his lips. "The party," he said, tugging her along as he strode toward a side corridor. "It's already in progress."

Carefully not looking at Leslie, Flint headed for wide double doors at the end of the passageway. She didn't matter to him, he assured himself, shaking off a crawly, confined feeling. At least she didn't matter in any meaningful way. His interest was purely physical—exciting, sensual, but purely physical. He might allow her to hold him momentarily but there was no way in hell he'd let her cage him. As he consciously reached for the oversized knob on the wide door, Flint unconsciously tightened his grip around the slender fingers entwined with his.

As Flint swung open the heavy door, Leslie had the sensation of being hit by a wall of sound. Combined music and laughter washed over her in a wave of noise, relieving the tension curling along her muscles and nerves. Leslie was not as a rule a party animal. Yet now she welcomed the clatter, chatter and bang attendant to the celebration. Suddenly she wanted to dance, she longed for a drink, but most of all she needed to remove herself from Flint Falcon for a while.

For the first few minutes after their arrival, chances seemed slim to none for Leslie to break free of Flint's grip. His expression benign yet remote, his handclasp firm, he made a slow circuit of the large ballroom, acknowledging calls of welcome from some, murmuring pleasantries to others, introducing Leslie to but a few.

Leslie's opportunity for escape came in the form of two men who simultaneously approached Flint from different directions. One of the men was a stranger to Leslie; the other was a blackjack dealer she recalled meeting in Las Vegas the previous fall. The stranger spoke softly to Flint, and the dealer spoke hesitantly to her.

"Miss Fairfield? I suppose you don't remember me, but..." The man's voice faded as Flint leveled a brooding, sharp-eyed look at him.

"Of course I remember you," Leslie said. "Dale Collins, isn't it?"

"Yes." Dale smiled with boyish pleasure, and sent a wary-eyed glance at Flint, who frowned.

Beginning to feel like Flint's possession, and resenting it, Leslie bristled inwardly but smiled brilliantly. "It's nice to see you again, Dale. You're working here now?" At his affirmative reply, she continued, "How do you like living on the east coast?"

Dale shrugged. "I really haven't been here long enough to tell." He laughed ruefully. "But my wife loves being so close to everything New York has to offer." Suddenly his eyes lit up. "We were in the audience the night of your last performance. It was terrific—my wife cried."

"Thank you." Leslie's smile was misty. "I cried too."

"I know." Dale hesitated, then said, "I know Jan would be thrilled to meet you. I don't suppose you'd—"

"Is your wife here tonight?" Leslie interrupted.

"Yes." Dale nodded and motioned to a small group of people seated at a table on the far side of the room. "Would you join us for a drink?"

If Flint had his priorities, so did Leslie; she knew the importance of personal contact with her fans. She didn't pause before responding. "I'd enjoy that." Turning to excuse herself, she felt her breath catch at the searing intensity of Flint's narrowed gaze.

"Going somewhere?" Flint inquired.

Leslie wasn't fooled by his mild tone; Flint was annoyed by Dale's offer and her acceptance of it. His attitude, along with the speculative interest of the man who had walked up to talk to him, rankled. Unused to having her actions questioned, Leslie grew rigid...and haughty. She returned his stare with sparks flaring from her green eyes.

"Yes." Leslie let the one clipped word convey her own annoyance. She'd planned to politely excuse herself and say she'd be right back. Instead she gave him a dismissive smile before turning to accompany Dale to his table.

Watching the smooth line of her gently swaying hips, Falcon experienced an unusual combination of emotions deep in his gut. He was feeling inordinately angry and oddly bereft. But there was another sensation as well—it was almost as if someone had taken his most valued possession. The feeling confused him, for though he wryly acknowledged his need to physically possess Leslie, he knew his *most* valued possession was his fiercely guarded freedom. Shying away from analyzing his feelings, Flint casually returned his attention to the man patiently waiting at his side.

Flint heard every word that the man, who happened to be the head of the hotel's security force, said to him. At the same time, his expression austere and unrevealing, Flint carefully monitored every move Leslie made, his response inward and concealed.

His lips burned when, after taking a sip of wine, the tip of her tongue flicked at a golden drop shimmering on her lip. His stomach muscles contracted when she laughed at something someone had said. His chest seemed to compress when she tossed her head to flip her flaming mass of hair off one shoulder. But, as he soon learned, the worst was yet to come.

Listening intently to his security chief and giving his usual short, terse replies, Flint felt every muscle in his body tighten when Leslie accompanied a member of Dale's party onto the dance floor. He felt offended by the smile on her lips; he felt murderous at the way she allowed the man to draw her too tightly into his arms; and as if she were pressed to him, he felt his body quicken and harden in response.

Flint was beginning to sweat where it didn't show by the time Leslie drifted back to him. "Enjoying the party?" he asked in a pleasant tone, restraining an urge to manacle her slender wrist with his strong fingers.

"Yes, they're nice people," Leslie said, raising her eyebrows as she glanced around. "Where is your friend?"

"He's not a friend; he works for me." Flint's dismissive tone ended the subject. "What was Collins talking about?" he asked, introducing another topic.

"When?" Leslie responded coolly, put off by his seeming disregard for an employee.

Leslie's distant tone sent fresh anger surging through Flint. Amazed at the difficulty he had controlling his temper, Falcon injected a note of casual interest into his low voice. "When he said that he and his wife were in the audience the night you gave your last performance."

"I'm an actress, Flint," she explained. "I decided to bow out of the play I was in when I realized it was going stale for me. Dale and his wife were in the audience the night of my last performance."

"How long were you a member of the cast?" Flint asked with interest.

"Not quite ten months." Leslie smiled. "I loved it, but I was beginning to feel tired, physically tired, and I thought I'd better withdraw gracefully before it showed in my performance."

Flint stared at her intently. "You're feeling all right now?" His voice, though low, had sharpened. "You're not ill?" Even to himself Flint could not have explained the darting pang of alarm he felt.

"I'm fine." Leslie laughed. "I've worked very hard and I needed a break, that's all." Her laughter subsiding, she gave him a pointed look. "I came to Atlantic City to play. Didn't you mention something about making a brief appearance at this party?"

A wry smile eased Flint's taut expression. "The casino doesn't open until tomorrow night," he said. "But I think I could find another kind of game to amuse you."

"Yes, I'm sure you could." Suppressing the excitement his insinuation generated, Leslie gave him a prim look and spun away, heading for the door. He was beside her within two strides, his hand curving about her waist in a proprietary way.

"Where are you going, Red?" he murmured at her ear.

Feeling suddenly young and bubbly and full of expectation, Leslie waited until they had swept from the ballroom before tilting her head to give him a sparkling gaze from her long eyes. Then, her lips almost brushing his jaw, she whispered, "Yours isn't the only game in town, Mr. Falcon."

Four

A gust of cold wind whipped off the ocean to sweep the boardwalk, swirling bits of paper debris into the air. Clamping one hand onto her wildly flying hair, Leslie burrowed her chin into her collar and silently thanked Flint for insisting they return to his apartment for her coat before leaving the hotel.

Deciding she needed some exercise and a lot of fresh air after the smoky warmth inside the ballroom, Leslie had opted to walk to the hotel-casino, which was situated at the far end of the boardwalk. With the realization of how cold the night wind had grown, she belatedly questioned the wisdom of her decision to walk. While one hand was warmly curled inside her coat pocket, the hand anchoring her hair was cold, as were her ears and the tip of her nose. They were still less than half the distance to their destination, and the fact that she was forced to stop every few feet to tug one or the other of the slim heels on her shoes from between the boards slowed their progress considerably. She was pondering on whether or not to request they stop at the casino they were closest to when Flint brought her to a halt by grasping her upper arm.

"Wait a minute," he said, turning her as he pivoted to put the wind at their backs.

Frowning, Leslie watched as he yanked a white silk scarf from around his neck, the single concession he'd made to ward off the chill of the late-fall evening while stoically insisting that she don her winter coat. When Leslie had taunted him about the scant protection the scarf would give him, Flint had shrugged and said, "I never mind the cold."

Now, as he released her arm to capture the flapping end of the scarf, Leslie was inclined to believe him. Flint didn't look cold or even chilly. His statement was further proved when, after sliding the scarf around her head, his warm fingers brushed the tender skin on the underside of her jaw as he looped one end over the other and tugged gently to fasten it.

"There." Stepping back, Flint cocked his head to survey his work. "That'll keep your hair from flying all over the place and keep your ears warm as well."

"Thank you, but now you have no protec—" Leslie's voice faded as she caught sight of two men from the corner of her eye. In itself, the presence of men on the boardwalk would not have caught her attention; there were many men and women strolling or rushing along the boards at all hours of the day and night, but Leslie had noticed these two particular men before, moments after she and Flint had left Falcon's Flight.

"Leslie?" Flint was obviously puzzled. "What's wrong?"

"I'm probably being imaginative, but..." Leslie smiled without conviction and lowered her voice. "Flint, I believe we're being followed by those men hovering over there." She indicated the two men with a brief movement of her head. Her eyes widened in disbelief at the pleasant sound of his soft laughter.

"I'll have to talk to my security chief; they're supposed to be inconspicuous."

"You mean they *are* following us!" Leslie gasped.

"Humm." He nodded once, then turned and continued walking, urging her along by pressing his palm to her back. "They're my bodyguards," he explained as she opened her mouth to question him.

"Bodyguards?" Leslie repeated, stunned and suddenly uneasy. "Why do you need bodyguards?"

"To protect my body," Flint replied. Then he added, "My back, primarily."

"What from?" she asked, fully aware of the stupidity of her question.

"Attack. Injury." Flint shrugged. "Whatever."

Great. Wonderful. Terrific. Leslie shivered as the thoughts tumbled through her mind. Out of all the males frequenting Atlantic City at this particular time, she had singled out a man who required the services of bodyguards! Fantastic. Of course, Leslie hastened to point out to herself, she hadn't exactly singled him out. Flint Falcon had *commandeered* her!

"It's nothing to go into fits over," Flint said, slanting a shrewd glance at her expression of consternation.

"I never have fits." Leslie's tone was repressive.

"Okay," he shot back with agreeable smoothness, "then it's nothing for you to be concerned about."

Stopping abruptly, Leslie whipped around to face him. "Really?" she said challengingly. "Since you pay for their services, I must assume you feel a need for the bodyguards. And if you feel that need, then I must assume there is plenty to be concerned about." She strode away from him, moving toward the entrance of the hotel that had been their destination. Flint's hand covered hers as she grasped the cold metal bar on the revolving door.

"Will you listen?" he muttered, pressing his chest to her back in the tiny wedge of space intended for one person. "I'm not concerned," he continued as they stepped together into the spacious lobby. "My security chief insisted on the guards." His shoulders moved in a dismissive shrug. "I tolerate them as long as they don't crowd me."

Moving toward the escalator that led to the casino, Leslie spared him a glowering over-the-shoulder glance. "There must be a reason your security chief insisted upon the guards," she said, her lips tightening in disapproval.

"Well, of course there is." Flint was losing patience, and it showed. "Leslie, use your head. I'm in a high-risk business. You knew that from the beginning."

So strong was the force of his stare that Leslie nearly missed stepping off the moving stairs when they'd reached the top. Flint's hands flashed out to steady her when she stumbled slightly. "Thank you," she muttered ungraciously, veering away from him. She didn't like it, not any of it. The thought of why he would need bodyguards upset and frightened her. But more than anything else, Leslie was angry.

She slowed her rapid steps as she approached a bank of dollar slot machines. Leslie felt Flint come to a stop beside her as she fumbled with the catch on her small evening bag. She snagged a nail and cursed in an undertone. Dammit! she wailed inwardly. First the escalator, now this stupid catch! How dare he say she knew he was in a high-risk business from the beginning? He had begun this...this whatever it was, not she!

"You're going to play the machines?" Flint's tone was heavy with disbelief, which merely added fuel to her anger.

"I'd say that was a pretty dumb question," she fairly snarled, "since I'm standing directly in front of one." The silence that ensued was infinitely more frightening than learning about his bodyguards. Already regretting her snide remark and the sharpness of her tone, Leslie suffered his cold silence in remorse.

"Don't push your luck, honey." Flint's voice was terrifying in its icy softness.

Feeling the chill to her toes, Leslie didn't have to be told that he was not referring to the machines or any other games of chance. Tension humming along her nerves, a cloying sense of fear pervading her being, she stood staring sightlessly at the three stilled reels behind the rectangular window on the slot machine. She came to the conclusion that for her Falcon was the biggest gamble in town. In her distraction, Leslie was unaware of her fingers picking at the purse clasp.

"Oh, for God's sake, here!" Pulling her hand away from the purse, Flint slapped a hundred-dollar bill into her palm. "Where did you get that bag, Wells Fargo?"

"I don't want your money, Falcon."

Flint ignored her low, gritty tone and the bill she shoved at him. "I've upset you."

Trying to collect herself, Leslie crumpled the bill as she curled her fingers into her palm. "Why would you think that?" she sniped in a saccharine tone.

"Leslie, I'm sorry. I—"

"*I* came to play, remember?" Leslie cut him off, simply because he didn't sound at all sorry. "And that's exactly what I'm going to do." Thinking, *The hell with it!* she held the bill aloft to catch the attention of the change person inside the bank of machines.

After exchanging the money for dollar tokens, Leslie dropped four of the wrapped rolls into the coin tray under a machine and rapped the fifth one sharply against its edge. When the large tokens spilled from the broken wrapper, she immediately fed three into the slot, then pulled the handle jerkily, aware of the man who was leaning against the machine.

The reels spun, then settled—click, click, click. Nothing. Leslie repeated the process several times with the same results. The greedy machine ate up the first roll of tokens and three-quarters of another without returning even the smallest of hits. Unconcerned, Leslie fed the voracious thing three more tokens.

"Heavens, this is exciting," Flint observed, yawning as she yanked on the handle.

Gritting her teeth to keep from telling him exactly where he could put his observations, Leslie glared at the whirling reels. Her teeth unclenched when the first reel stopped with the double bar on the center pay line. Her breath quickened when the second reel came to a matching halt. Her expression grew superior as the third double bar lined up. Bells rang and the light on top of the machine lit up as the machine began spitting out the payoff of one hundred and fifty tokens. Turning casually, Leslie smiled at Flint. "Actually, I do find it rather exciting, but if you're bored, please feel free to do whatever excites you." She raised a hand and moved it to indicate the room.

Flint was not without humor, and he proved it with a bark of delighted laughter. "Point taken," he drawled, pushing himself upright. "Tell you what," he continued, "if you're going to play the machines awhile, there is someone here I'd like to talk to, not that that will be any more exciting." He arched an eyebrow quizzically.

Leslie smiled. "Yes, I'm going to play."

"Okay, suppose we meet at the coffee shop in, say, an hour and a half?" Again his eyebrows peaked questioningly.

"Fine." Leslie checked her watch.

Leslie absently scooped tokens from the tray as she watched Flint walk away, his back straight, his head held at a high, superior angle. Flint Falcon was certainly worth the watching, she decided, in more ways than one. Expelling a soft sigh, she turned back to the machine when she lost sight of him.

As a rule, as she had explained to her friend Marie, Leslie could lose herself, shrug off all her nagging cares and considerations, by immersing herself in casino play. But for some reason that evening proved to be the exception. Once started, it seemed the machine was hell-bent on depositing every token in its drum into the coin tray. All manner of bar combinations aligned on the payoff line—a phenomenon that generally would have fascinated Leslie. But, though the tray filled to the edge with tokens, Leslie just couldn't work up much enthusiasm.

It was all Flint Falcon's fault, she mused dejectedly, transferring the tokens from the tray to a large plastic container supplied by the change attendant. She'd come to Atlantic City to unwind, and thoughts of Flint had her more keyed up than she'd been in weeks, or maybe months, or even forever!

Bodyguards, for heaven's sake! Leslie thought, barely noticing the crush of people as she carried the heavy container to the coin-exchange window. What was she doing with a man who required bodyguards? she asked herself, watching disinterestedly as a casino employee dumped the tokens into a counting machine and numbers started mounting on the attached device. Even when the numbers stopped to reveal a total of six hundred and seventy-two dollars, Leslie couldn't dredge up more than a faint smile. She did, however, respond politely when the employee offered his congratulations along with the crisp bills he very carefully counted out before sliding them across the counter to her.

Now what? Leslie wondered, desultorily stashing the bills into her purse. Glancing at her watch, she sighed, then went still as the soft sound registered on her astounded mind. She was bored! She, Leslie Fairfield, the woman known to derive delight and genuine release from tension by playing at the games of chance, was bored, and she had barely started! And all because of a man! It was downright demoralizing.

Drifting along the aisles in the slot-machine section, occasionally dodging a cluster of people grouped around a single machine, Leslie pondered her distracting problem—namely, Flint Falcon—and exactly how she had managed to get herself into such a predicament in the first place.

For a time, Leslie tried to deny responsibility by maintaining she'd had little choice in the matter; Flint had literally swooped down on her the instant she'd stepped into his blasted hotel. But honesty wouldn't allow her to continue thinking along that line, simply because she knew she had the option of walking away from him.

So, Leslie asked herself as she moved toward the table games, why not walk away from him?

She quickly answered her silent query. Flint Falcon was the most interesting man she had run across in years—not to mention the single sexiest man she had *ever* run across! Leslie sighed again and accepted the fact that she wanted to be with Flint in every sense of the term *be with*.

Okay, so accept all of it, Leslie silently advised herself, pausing a few moments to watch the play at a crowded, noisy craps table. Accept his forcefulness, the dark aura of power surrounding him, the unsettling sense of frightening excitement that emanates from him *and* the damned bodyguards.

Moving away from the table, Leslie didn't even hear the shout of victory from a man who had tossed the dice for an important win. She was too involved with listening to the thundering sound of her own increased heartbeat for, having once again glanced at her watch, she realized it was time to meet her fate—in the dark form of Flint Falcon.

Flint was waiting for her, propped with deceptive indolence against the coffee-shop wall. He had been waiting for thirty-odd minutes. Impatience abraded Flint's nerves, impatience with Leslie and with himself, but mostly with the inner need he felt for her, a need that had been growing at a steady rate into a voracious hunger.

Although Flint had sought out the man he'd wanted to talk to, in actual time he hadn't spent more than ten minutes conversing with him. Flint had filled the long interval by wandering around the huge casino, his expression forbidding as he fought a silent, inner struggle with himself.

The conflict within Flint was at his most basic, most vulnerable level. In some insidious way, a way Flint couldn't—or wouldn't—as yet comprehend, his emotions were getting all tangled up with his desires in regards to Leslie Fairfield. And try as he might to dismiss other than physical considerations of her, his wary emotions kept getting in the way.

Leslie was just another in a long line of women, Flint told himself repeatedly while strolling from the tables to the machines and back to the tables again. And, though his piercing gaze swept the faces of the assortment of females, he also repeatedly assured himself he wasn't looking for one female face in particular.

By the time Flint propped his body against the coffee-shop wall, he was ready to admit to a feeling of testy impatience. He was also ready to admit that he had been lying to himself. And by the time he spotted Leslie drifting toward him, looking as delicious and inviting as an oasis in the middle of a scorched, parched desert, he was ready to admit that Leslie was not just another in a long line of women. Flint wasn't ready to examine, never mind admit to, why he felt differently about Leslie.

Freedom, his own personal freedom, headed the list of values in Flint Falcon's life; all others came below it in order of their importance. If necessary, Flint was prepared to fight, even die, to maintain his freedom. Yet since meeting Leslie, since *wanting* Leslie, his sense of absolute freedom had felt strangely threatened. Therein lay the cause of Flint's inner conflict. Flint wanted his freedom. Flint also wanted Leslie. He resolved the inner war by convincing himself he'd have both—his freedom on a permanent basis, Leslie temporarily. Pleased by the resolution, Flint greeted Leslie with a smile and felt every muscle in his body contract when she smiled back.

"Did you win?"

Unable to avoid applying his question to her struggle with her doubts about her association with him as well as to her gambling luck, Leslie's smile slipped into a satisfied grin. "Yes. Did you locate the man you wanted to talk to?"

"Yes." Flint inclined his head to indicate the coffee shop. "Would you like a cup of coffee?" When Leslie answered with a quick negative shake of her head, he said, "Would you like to go into one of the lounges for a drink?"

"No, thank you," she replied, waiting for whatever he suggested next.

Flint's eyes narrowed slightly. "Would you like to go on to another casino?"

"No." Leslie smiled and waited, feeling excitement begin to hum along her veins at the speculative expression that came into his face.

"Would you like to return to Falcon's Flight?" Although he didn't add "and to my apartment—and my bedroom," he really didn't need to; the suggestion was woven through his low, sensual voice. Leslie didn't hesitate an instant.

"Yes," she said at once, tired of the games.

It was not until Leslie was standing on the broad landing inside the apartment, breath suspended in awe as she gazed at the panoramic sweep of star-studded night sky afforded by the window wall, that she gave a thought to the bodyguards.

"What happened to your shadows?" she asked, her breathing resuming at an alarming rate as Flint set the lock on the door.

"I told them to catch the next available cab," he murmured, sliding his hand beneath the heavy mass of her hair as he came up behind her.

"I'll bet that made them happy." Leslie shivered at the feather-light touch of his fingers on her nape. The shiver intensified at the sound of his soft chuckle.

"It probably didn't, but I sure as hell wasn't about to share our cab with them." His free hand slid around her waist, drawing her tingling spine into contact with his hard chest. "Forget them, darling. They're experts. They won't bother you."

"Merely knowing they're around bothers me," Leslie sighed, savoring his endearment as she let her head rest against his solid strength.

"They're not here," Flint murmured at her ear. "We're completely alone." He touched the tip of his tongue to her temple. "Or does that bother you even more?"

Leslie was too honest to be less than forthright. "I won't insult your intelligence by lying to you, Flint." She shivered again as his tongue stroked the skin at her hairline. "I am—" she swallowed a gasp as his palm moved slowly over her rib cage "—nervous about this arrangement."

"Why?" Flint's tone was tinged with genuine puzzlement. His hand found one already aching breast and felt the evidence of arousal in the hardening crest. "We're both mature, experienced adults," he reasoned. "What is there for you to be nervous about?"

Leslie closed her eyes as his hand grasped her hair to expose her nape, and bit back a moan when his lips caressed the vulnerable skin. "I—I'm unaccustomed to indulging in affairs," she gasped, shuddering in response to his fingers stroking the taut material shielding her breast. "Besides that fact, I haven't been with a man in over a year," she admitted in a breathless rush. "And I'm feeling more than a little uncertain about what I'm doing here."

Flint went still for a moment before, stepping back, he turned her to face him. "Why?" His voice combined amazement and curiosity.

Thinking he referred to the last part of her explanation, she said, "I told you, I'm unaccustomed..." Her voice faded as he shook his head.

"I don't mean that," he said, dismissing her attempt at elaboration. "Why haven't you been with a man in over a year?"

Surprised by the tight, oddly excited inflection in his voice, Leslie stared at him in utter confusion. His impatient "Answer me!" brought her to her senses.

"Because I went through a rather nasty divorce a year ago," she snapped, whirling away from him to descend the stairs into the living room. As she neared the center of the large room, Leslie felt him behind her and she spun around to face him again. "I haven't been having particularly kind thoughts about men in general during the past year," she said, revealing hidden bitterness she had thought she'd put behind her. She tried a careless shrug and failed miserably. "Unkind thoughts are not conducive to love affairs," she said, smiling dryly, "which I'm unaccustomed to indulging in, anyway."

The sensuous mood was broken, at least temporarily. Leslie knew it and, judging by his expression, so did Flint. His lips slanting in a wry smile, he sauntered to the ornately carved credenza.

"Can I get you a drink?" he asked, opening the long cabinet to reveal a well-stocked bar and a small refrigerator.

"Will I need it?" Leslie's question earned her a flashing grin from Flint, a grin so blatantly sexy she suddenly tensed with anticipation again.

"If you mean as fortification to face what is definitely going to happen later, then no, you don't need it." Flint's grin softened into a smile. "There's no hurry, Leslie. We have all the time you require. Now can I get you a drink?"

"Will you be joining me?"

"Of course."

"Then yes, please. I'll have a glass of white wine."

After pouring out two glasses of wine, Flint led Leslie to the long couch positioned in front of the window wall. He waited until she was comfortably seated, then handed her a glass before sitting down beside her and draping his arm around her shoulders. Sipping the wine, Leslie steeled herself for the questions about her marriage and subsequent divorce that she felt positive were coming. She nearly choked on her wine when Flint finally spoke.

"So tell me," he invited softly, "what do you think of the view?"

Sputtering, laughing, Leslie cradled her wineglass protectively and stared into his gleaming dark eyes. He is a devil, she decided, catching her breath, an enchanting, beguiling devil of a man. And all the more dangerous for it!

"The view is spectacular and you know it." Leslie's voice revealed the delight she found in him; somehow she didn't care.

Flint obviously did care. The deep, exciting sound of his appreciative laughter was nearly her undoing. "Of course I know the view's spectacular," he admitted, "but the question did break the tension, didn't it?"

"Okay, I give up." Emitting a dramatic sigh, she settled in for the inquisition. "What do you want to know?"

"Everything," Flint responded immediately, surprising himself more than her. "Start at the beginning and take it from there."

Giving him a prim look, Leslie projected herself into the role of a young girl, about to render her first public recitation. "I was born thirty-seven years ago in a small town in—'' That was as far as he allowed her to go.

"Leslie." Flint's voice was low and tinged with amusement, but it also held a hint of warning. Leslie decided on prudence and took the hint.

"I always wanted to be a stage actress," she said abruptly. "I wanted it so much I could sometimes taste it." She paused in case he cared to comment, but Flint merely nodded. For some ridiculous reason, Leslie felt gratified by his understanding. After moistening her dry throat with a sip of wine, she went on, "I never even missed, let alone minded, the sacrifices made in pursuit of my dream. I rarely dated, I seldom went to parties or other social functions, I didn't go to college and I never even considered marriage until I was thirty-two years old." Again she waited for a comment from him; again Flint had none to make. "By the time I met *him* I was established, reasonably successful, more than financially solvent and a prime pushover for a golden-haired, godlike actor capable of wringing tears from an audience with his delivery of Hamlet's soliloquy." This time when Leslie paused, Flint did have a comment, which consisted of one succinct word.

"Him?"

"Bradford Quarrels, the theatrical darling of New York and London," Leslie said wryly, "and the boy wonder of almost any lady's bedroom." Her smile was self-mocking. "The first fact I knew before I met him."

"And the second fact?" Flint prompted.

"I refused to acknowledge until the day he told me he was leaving me." Leslie frowned into her glass. The wine was getting to her, inducing a heaviness in her limbs and eyelids. She yawned delicately before adding, "Brad's confession of infidelity was the final in a series of stunning blows."

"Blows?"

Leslie blinked at him. How, she wondered, had Flint managed to convey such tightly controlled fury in the utterance of one small word? The answer sprang into her mind even as the question was unrolling. "Oh! I didn't mean physical blows," she hastened to assure him. "Brad never raised a hand to me." Her smile was faint. "It probably would have been easier to take if he had . . . bruises heal rather quickly."

Flint's eyes narrowed. "I think you'd better explain that."

Leslie felt tired and sleepy. She didn't want to dredge it all up again, relive the hurtful memories, but Flint was staring—no, glaring—at her, waiting, and she knew he'd persist until she told him everything. Her sigh was soft but heartfelt.

"He is really an excellent actor, you know. He told me that the only time I was interesting and attractive was while I was onstage, playing a role. He said I was an uninspired and uninspiring partner in bed, which accounted for his need to seek excitement elsewhere, beginning with the second day of our honeymoon." Leslie tried to smile; the effort defeated her.

"And you believed him?" Flint's voice was raw with disbelief and anger.

"At the time, yes." Flint opened his mouth, but Leslie forestalled his protest. "Please try to understand," she pleaded. "I loved and trusted him. I had convinced myself that we were the perfect match—a meeting of minds, talent and emotions. I completely believed the part he had chosen to play for me . . . that of charming, intelligent, companionable friend and lover. I bought the whole nine yards. The occasional hints dropped in the trade papers I dismissed as vicious gossip, and although most of my friends knew the philandering bastard Brad really was, they thought to shield me by keeping silent. So yes, Flint, I believed every word and for a while I was devastated."

"What did you do?" Flint's voice was so soft, so gentle, it brought tears to her eyes.

"I fell apart and ran away." Leslie blinked again.

"Where did you run to?"

"To the same place and person I'd been running to all my life whenever I needed help." Leslie managed a genuine if weary smile. "I have an older cousin. He has always been my friend and champion." She laughed softly in remembrance. "He offered to go to New York and relieve Brad of his skin, a narrow strip at a time."

"Sounds to me like your cousin's got his priorities straight," Flint observed in dry agreement. "But of course you wouldn't allow it?"

"Of course not," Leslie concurred, settling her head against the back of the sofa. "But I must admit I was tempted." Her voice had lowered to a sleepy murmur.

"I must admit, so am I."

"He's not worth the effort. You'd only dirty your hands on the slimy jerk." Leslie lost the battle against her heavy eyelids. A soft sigh breathed through her lips as her body relaxed. The glass in her fingers tilted precariously. "I had heard that confession was good for the soul," she muttered. "But I had no idea it was so very exhausting."

"Careful, Red," Flint murmured, plucking the glass from her limp hand, "you don't want to stain that dress."

Leslie was poised on the edge of sleep, teetering uncertainly. She had the vague feeling that she should remain alert, she just couldn't remember why. Flint resolved her dilemma in the most comforting way; he drew her into the protective warmth of his arms. She heard his voice as if from a great distance as she snuggled into a deeper embrace.

"Sleep, darling. Nothing will hurt you here," Flint whispered against her silky hair. "Not even me."

Five

Leslie came awake slowly to the luxurious feeling of warm comfort and the tantalizing aroma of fresh coffee. Inhaling deeply, she freed her arms from the covers and stretched them over her head, murmuring an appreciative "Humm."

"Good morning."

The soft greeting brought Leslie fully alert. Blinking, she focused on the tall man standing by the unfamiliar bed, his long hands curled around steaming cups. Her heartbeat fluttering into a rapid tattoo, she pulled her gaze from Flint's sardonic expression and glanced around the enormous room.

Where was she? Leslie wondered, frowning. More to the point, how did she get to wherever she was? And even more to the point, what, if anything, had happened between the last she remembered in the living room and now? The answer to her initial question was obvious, even to Leslie's sleepy mind. Her gaze shot back to Flint.

"You're in my bed, in my room," he said, confirming her conclusion.

"But how..." Leslie's voice failed as he moved to stand by the bed and held one of the cups out to her. "How did I get here?" she continued, frowning up at him.

"I carried you." Flint smiled wryly at her. "Are you going to sit up?"

"Yes, but..." she began, envisioning the curving staircase.

"Drink first, talk later." Flint's sardonic expression dissolved into real, heart-wrenching tenderness. "But to set your mind at rest so you can drink, I'll assure you that you're as untouched now as you were when you fell asleep in my arms last night."

Accepting his word without a shred of doubt, Leslie wiggled to sit up. The covers fell to her waist, revealing her lacy bra. She arched her eyebrows at him as she reached for the cup.

Flint answered her silent query with a question. "You would have preferred to sleep in your dress?" Sitting down next to her, he stared openly at her barely concealed breasts.

Leslie had the uncanny sensation that she could feel his intense gaze; she *knew* she felt the heat from it all the way to her flushed cheeks. "No, of course not," she finally replied in a dry, crackly voice. Lifting the cup, she gulped the hot coffee.

"Your former husband was a fool," Flint said, raising his eyes to capture her shifting gaze. "You're a beautiful woman, Leslie." He smiled and tilted his cup in a silent salute.

His praise sent pleasure radiating through her to deepen the flush on her cheeks and put a gleam in her exotic eyes. "Thank you, Flint," Leslie murmured. "You're beautiful, too."

Flint's laughter poured through the room like sparkling sun rays. "No, Leslie, I'm not beautiful." His teeth flashed in a devilish grin. "I face the beast in the mirror every morning, and I have yet to be confronted by beauty." He shook his head to silence her when she opened her mouth to protest. "But I like hearing it just the same," he admitted with amused candor. "Now drink your coffee before it gets cold."

Unused to taking orders, Leslie stared at him a moment before lowering her gaze to examine his body with frank appraisal. The act of defiance backfired. Leslie felt the heat of sensual arousal suffuse her body at the overwhelming male look of him. Attired casually in a sweater that clung to his broad, flatly muscled chest and brushed-suede slacks that hugged his narrow waist and hips, Flint was most definitely all male. The mere sight of him rattled her senses and loosened her tongue.

"You're wrong, you know," she breathed, raising her bemused gaze to his. "You are one beautiful man." As her gaze met and tangled with his, all the air seemed to rush out of Leslie's body. There was a stillness about him that made her shiver. His strange eyes had darkened to near black. There was a tremor in the strong fingers that gripped the coffee cup. Leslie tensed as he carefully set the cup on an intricately carved nightstand by the bed, and stopped breathing when he took her cup from her to set it next to his. "Flint?" The voice that projected so effectively from any stage was now reedy and faint.

"Don't be frightened. I won't hurt you." His hands settled on her shoulders, fingers flexing gently into her soft flesh. His movements were slow, unhurried, as he drew her to him. "I know it's been a while for you." His low, exciting voice enveloped her senses as he embraced her trembling body. "Your flattery, however innocently meant, was wildly arousing," he murmured, brushing his parted lips over her cheek. "I want the mouth that gave me the compliment."

"Flint."

His mouth claimed her parted lips sweetly, masterfully, completely, and evoked a hunger unlike anything Leslie had ever before experienced. Suddenly starving for his unique taste, she curled her arms around his neck and fed greedily from his mouth. When his tongue slid along her lower lip, she tightened her arms and opened her mouth fully in invitation. Leslie heard Flint's low growl with every one of her senses and felt the spearing thrust of his tongue to the heart of her femininity. When he ended the kiss, she murmured in protest.

"I know, I want more too." His breathing uneven, Flint held her away from him to stare into her eyes. "I want it all," he said, his voice a harsh contrast to the gentle stroke of his fingers on her warm skin. "If you're unsure, tell me now, while I still have control."

Leslie's hands were resting on his shoulders. Responding silently, she slid her hands down his chest to tug at the hem of his sweater. It was all the invitation

Flint required. Within seconds the floor was littered with clothes and Flint was sliding his body next to hers on the bed.

Shivering from a mixture of uncertainty and anticipation, Leslie moaned softly when Flint brought her nipples to tight arousal with repeated flicks of his tongue, and cried her pleasure aloud when he closed his lips on one tight bud to suckle hungrily.

Needing to touch him, Leslie stroked Flint's smooth warm skin from his shoulders to his tight buttocks, her own pleasure increasing every time he gasped or groaned in response. Each time his lips returned to hers, his kiss was more demanding, more urgent. Leslie gave her mouth willingly and arched her body in offering.

When Flint finally accepted her offering, he did so with care. His movement slow, his gaze fastened to her face for the smallest twinge of discomfort, he made himself a part of her and her a part of him. Then he paused to allow her body to adjust to the fullness of his need. Bending to her, he kissed her and continued to kiss her until, on fire for him, Leslie initiated the motion by arching her hips into his.

Tension coiled inside Leslie, tighter and tighter, spiraling up to reduce her breathing to ragged gasps and push a low, whimpering sound from her throat. Flint was like liquid fire, washing over her, drowning her in a flood of searing sensuousness.

His body taut with the same coiling tightness, Flint drove himself to the edge of reason. He didn't want the tension to end, not ever, yet his body shivered with anticipation of joyous release. Leslie's soft, throaty cries excited him unbearably, driving him wild with the desire to give her more pleasure than he derived himself. His body was damp, his muscles taut with strain when he felt her body contract around him an instant before Leslie cried his name. With an unfamiliar sense of awe, Flint savored the pulsating shudders cascading through her body.

And still Flint held back, gritting his teeth as he maintained his cadence, striving to increase her pleasure, needing to prove her own sensuality to her. Dragging air into his burning chest, he gathered the last of his strength and thrust his hips into hers. Flint's reward was twofold. Leslie's body contracted again and her long nails scored his back as she sobbed his name. The sound of her voice shattered him into flaming pieces of unbelievable, almost painful pleasure. No longer able to think, breathe or even move physically, Flint experienced the most incredible sensation of taking flight spiritually. For one perfect instant, the feeling of soaring freedom was exquisite. Then, slowly, deliciously, he glided back to a soft landing against Leslie's heaving breasts.

Leslie was barely aware of the weight of Flint's body; she felt stunned. Never, never would she have believed in the possibility of such excruciating pleasure or her own ability to attain it. Awareness came as her breathing leveled and her rioting heartbeat slowed. Still keyed to a trembling pitch, Leslie raised her hands to stroke and caress the man responsible for her double burst of ecstasy. Like her own, Flint's muscles were quivering in reaction to the release from strain. Her hands moved lightly over his moist skin, smoothing, soothing the tension. She sighed when Flint reciprocated, stroking her trembling body from shoulder to thigh. She sighed again as she settled down, replete, complete, content. But she was tired, so very tired. Leslie's eyelids drifted shut to the lullaby of Flint's gentle murmurings.

"You are the sleepingest woman." Flint's teasing voice drew her from that gray plane between wakefulness and sleep.

Leslie's lips curved into a satisfied smile. "What time is it?" she murmured, putting off the moment of opening her eyes.

"It's after one, and you've been sleeping—" he paused tellingly "—off and on for over thirteen hours. It's past lunch and we haven't even had breakfast."

Leslie covered her mouth and yawned. "Are you hungry?"

"Yes. Aren't you?"

"Umm, but I was so tired." Leslie yawned again. "Is sleepingest really a word or did you just coin it?" She opened her eyes to the thrill of gazing into his. Flint was lying on his side, his torso propped up on one elbow, his head resting on his closed hand.

"Who cares?" He smiled down at her and moved his shoulder in a half shrug. "But you are not only the sleepingest woman," he went on in a lowered tone, "you are a magnificent woman."

"Oh, Flint!" Leslie could say no more; emotion welled within her. She swallowed hard several times, then tried again. "But it wasn't me, it was—"

"I changed my mind," he said, cutting off her attempt at words. "Your former husband is not a fool, he's a blithering idiot and a liar to boot."

Leslie's eyes filled with hot tears. He didn't need to elaborate; she understood and was gratified by what he was trying to convey to her. Brad had excused his own reprehensible behavior by accusing her of inadequacy, an inadequacy that Flint now denied. She had given Flint Falcon pleasure. Leslie's spirit sang with the realization. Lifting her hand, she trailed her fingers over the skin stretched tautly on his face. "Thank you," she whispered, ignoring the tears trickling down her temples. "But it was you, Flint, don't you see? You made it magnificent for me."

A spasm of emotion passed over his face, a fleeting expression almost like fear. Then it was gone, and he smiled at her. "I have never known such pleasure with any other woman, Leslie," he confessed in a hesitant, oddly hoarse voice.

Overwhelmed and delighted by his admission, Leslie slid her fingers into his dark hair and drew his face down to hers. "The pleasure was mine, Mr. Falcon," she murmured, molding her mouth to his.

His kiss was deep and dark and every bit as exciting as before. His hands were warm, his fingers electrifying as they sought every pleasure spot on her body. Incredibly, unbelievably, Leslie was aroused within minutes—wildly, abandonedly aroused. While her mouth was devouring and being devoured and her tongue engaged his in dueling play, her hands caressed his long, finely honed body.

"Yes, yes," Flint moaned into her mouth as her fingers scored up along his taut thighs. "Oh, Leslie, yes!" he groaned when she closed her hand around him.

Leslie felt buoyant with a sense of power. Caressing him, teasing him, testing his strength was not only exciting but exhilarating. Flint's uninhibited response fired her passion, spurring her on to even more intimate caresses.

"Enough!" Catching her around the waist, Flint drew her body over his. His lips roamed her face before fastening on to her open mouth. His fingers flexed into her rounded bottom. Slowly, carefully, he drew her up. "See what you've done?" he whispered, nipping at her lips, then her throat, then her shoulders. Then, just as slowly, just as carefully, he drew her down, sheathing himself inside her. Clasping her by the hips, he initiated a rocking cadence. "Show me your magnificence, Leslie," he groaned, arching his body into hers. "Pleasure me. Let me pleasure you."

It had happened again. His nostrils flaring as he dragged air into his body, Flint stared at the high, slanted ceiling and examined the thought. That fantastic sensation of soaring free had again been achieved on finding release. The sensation could very likely become addictive, Flint thought. He also thought it more than strange that he'd never experienced the sensation with another woman—and at the age of forty, he'd known his share.

A murmur and a stirring beside him shattered Flint's introspection. A smile relieving the normal austerity of his face, he turned to gaze into eyes the color of a misty glen.

"Are you going to sleep again?"

"No." Leslie sighed her content. "I'd like to, but I must go to the bathroom." She gave him a rakish grin. "Want to join me?"

"Are you trying to kill me, woman?" Flint scowled. "It is now after two. I haven't eaten since dinner last night. I'm hungry." His statement came on a low growl.

"Okay, but never say you didn't have the chance." Her grin unrepentant, Leslie slid off the bed. She took three steps, glanced around, then turned to look at him, eyebrows raised. "Where is the bathroom?"

"Through the door to your left." Flint indicated the mirrored door with an idle wave of his hand while his narrow gaze took slow inventory of her enticing figure. Moving with purpose, he sat up and swung his long legs to the floor. "Maybe I'll change my mind," he said, his glittering gaze climbing back up her body to her flushed face, "and join you in there."

Leslie took to her heels. "Too late," she called back, dashing into the bathroom and locking the door behind her. "You can do something about rustling up some food," she said, raising her voice to penetrate the solid wood panel.

"You may be great in bed, but you're a nag, woman!" Flint yelled back at her and she heard a burst of delightful-sounding male laughter.

Great in bed. Leslie smiled smugly at her reflection in the long mirror above the sink cabinets. The image smiled back for a moment; then the smile faded. As a compliment, "great in bed" was a good one, she supposed, coming from a man as experienced as Falcon obviously was. But it sure didn't say much about what he thought of her as a person.

A frown tugging her eyebrows together, Leslie moved to the enormous sunken tub and reached down to twist the gold faucets. Gold? Her frown giving way to amazement, Leslie peered at the intricately carved knobs. They had been fashioned into the likeness of falcons' heads, and they looked as if they were made of solid gold!

"Good grief!" Leslie whispered in an awed tone. Forgetting her conflicting emotions over his dubious compliment, she examined the room.

And the room was certainly interesting. In fact, it was fascinating. Sybaritic. The word sprang into Leslie's mind as she stared at the gold-veined black marble tub, walls and floor. A contrasting gold-veined white marble topped the vanity sink cabinets that ran the entire length of one wall. Gold scrolled the frosted glass enclosing the separate shower stall which, Leslie discovered upon inspection, was roomy enough to accommodate at least half a dozen people comfortably.

It would seem that Flint Falcon certainly enjoyed more than his share of creature comforts, Leslie mused, deciding to forego the luxury of wallowing in the sunken tub for the novelty of a shower stall that was the size of a dressing room.

Stepping out from under the delicious pulsating shower spray, Leslie realized she had a small problem. Dripping onto a fluffy white bath mat, she belatedly remembered that her clothes were elsewhere. "Oh, hell!" she groaned aloud, reaching for what had to be the largest bath sheet she'd ever seen. Sighing with resignation, she dried her body, then wrapped the terry sheet around herself like a sarong. She was about to leave when a light tap sounded on the door.

"Leslie, breakfast has arrived," Flint called. "And I have a robe for you."

Cracking the door a few inches, Leslie stuck her hand through the narrow opening and wiggled her fingers. She heard Flint chuckle an instant before she felt soft material draped over her arm. "Coward," he taunted as she pulled her arm back and shut the door.

A wry smile tilted her lips when she looked at the garment. It was made of velvet and was a brilliant shade of emerald green. It was definitely a woman's robe and obviously expensive. It had not come from among her things in the guest room closet. Did it belong to an ex-lover of Flint's? she wondered. Or did he simply keep a supply on hand to accommodate any woman who happened to drop in for the night?

On closer examination, Leslie realized that the robe was brand-new—not through any fantastic deductive power on her part, but simply because he'd forgotten to snip off a tiny size tag on the inside of the right sleeve. The size was her own.

First jewelry, then clothing, she thought, biting back a curse. The traditional gifts given to a—Leslie gritted her teeth.

Unwinding the towel, Leslie tossed it to the floor and glared at the robe before slipping into the enveloping warmth of fine velvet. The wide lapels and sleeve cuffs were trimmed with satin braid. Slash pockets were set into the side seams of the full skirt. The ends of the broad sash belt were satin-fringed. It was heavy. It was flagrantly luxurious. Leslie loved it.

Flint had said she was great in bed, Leslie reflected, eyeing her reflection wryly. Was the robe intended as payment for services rendered? Her expression soured at the unpalatable consideration. She ought to tear the thing from her body and throw it in his face, she fumed. She didn't require or want his gifts as compensation for pleasure received!

But the robe did complement her hair and eyes. Tilting her head, Leslie ran her gaze down the slender length of her mirrored image. The dressing gown suited her. Maybe she wouldn't throw it in his face after all.

"Leslie!" Impatience roughened Flint's raised voice.

"Yes!" Leslie called, grimacing at her reflection. "I'll be there in a minute." Nodding suddenly, decisively, she pulled the belt tight, slip knotted it, then reached for the doorknob. Her mind was made up; she'd keep the robe, at least as long as she remained in his apartment.

Pausing a second, she frowned into the mirror; her hair was a disheveled mess, the tangled strands a direct result of wild lovemaking. Well, hadn't she as much as promised herself a blazing affair during her vacation? Leslie chided herself, raking her fingers through the auburn mass. Yes, she acknowledged, she had promised not only herself but Marie as well. She'd even managed to find the tall, dark devil of a man to have an affair with—or, more correctly, the devil had found her.

Turning the doorknob, Leslie concluded she really had no reason to be affronted. Flint Falcon knew the rules of the affair game even if she didn't. And, since Flint had already proved to be a genial companion as well as an exciting, inspiring devil of a lover, she'd play by his rules until her vacation was over or the game was played out—whichever came first.

Squaring her shoulders, Leslie swung the door open and swept into the bedroom—when she wanted to, Leslie could sweep with the world's best sweepers—wearing the robe and a smile. But behind the smile she felt a pang of something strangely like remorse. She'd wanted this time with Flint almost from their first meeting. Why should she feel like a child denied the right to play in the sunshine?

The answer was in Flint's admiring expression. It would end sooner or later, and she would leave him. And that was the way she wished it, wasn't it? No commitments? No ties? Of course it was, Leslie assured herself. She slid onto a chair set opposite Flint's at the table that had been positioned in front of the expanse of windows. She had been the commitment route, and she was not a slow learner. In Leslie's opinion, once burned was once too often.

So why did the feeling of being denied sunlight persist? Why indeed? Shaking out her napkin, Leslie carefully laid it across her lap and attempted to put her queries and doubts to rest. She had come away to rest and play; she fully intended to do both.

"Are you going to eat it or glare at it?"

Leslie's head snapped up. "What?"

Flint gave her his now-familiar wry smile. "Your food," he explained, inclining his head to indicate her breakfast. "You haven't even removed the covers from the dishes, yet you're glaring at them as if they offend you."

"I'm sorry, I was—eh—thinking." Leslie managed a faint smile as she lifted the largest of the domed covers. "It looks delicious."

"It is." Flint motioned to his nearly empty plate. "At least it was when it was hot." His pause was brief. "What were you thinking about?"

Having taken a forkful of fluffy scrambled eggs into her mouth, Leslie finished eating, using the seconds to come up with a suitable reply. "The casino. Wasn't it supposed to open today?"

"It's open now."

"And you missed the grand opening?" Leslie sighed, feeling oddly at fault.

Flint shook his head. "No, Leslie, I didn't miss it. I was there when the casino was officially opened for business."

"But...how?" Leslie frowned. "I thought you were here." She glanced at the rumpled bed, then back at him.

Flint picked up the glass coffee carafe and refilled her cup and his own before responding. "I'm a night person, Leslie, nocturnal by nature." His lips slanted into a sardonic smile. "I wasn't at all tired when you fell asleep last night. So after I put you to bed I went to my office." He moved his head to indicate a door in the wall opposite the bathroom. "I worked until three; *then* I joined you in bed."

"But didn't the casino open at ten?"

Flint nodded. "Of course. I slept my usual four hours, then went back into my office until it was time for the grand opening."

"I see," she said, beginning to believe that what she really saw was a dynamic, very purposeful man. Leslie pushed aside her half-finished meal and raised her eyebrows as she sipped on the hot coffee. "You only ever sleep four hours at a time?"

"Generally." Flint's smile was suggestive. "There are exceptions to every rule, of course." His tone, plus his smile, left little doubt in her mind as to what those exceptions were.

"Of course," she murmured dryly.

Flint's smile deepened. "Any other questions?"

"Yes." Leslie smoothed her palm over the velvet. "About this robe you handed to me..."

"What about it?" One dark eyebrow slanted arrogantly.

"It isn't mine," she chided softly.

"It is now." Flint's tone hardened warningly; Leslie chose to ignore it.

"I do not require payment, Flint," she said, bristling. "I thought I'd made that clear last night."

Flint had been lounging in the padded chair. As she spoke he slowly sat up straight. "I didn't buy the jewelry or the robe as a form of payment, Leslie." His voice sliced at her like cold steel. "I never *pay* for services rendered." Sheer male arrogance defined the tilt of his head. "And I never explain my motives to anyone." His smile was remote, chilling. "I will make an exception in this case, but I will tell you once and only once. I bought the gifts because it pleased me to do so. Is that completely understood?"

Not even to herself could Leslie deny the sense of intimidation his attitude and drilling stare sent streaking through her. But she wouldn't have admitted to the sensation under threat of bodily injury.

NO COST! NO OBLIGATION!
NO PURCHASE NECESSARY!

PLAY "LUCKY 7"
AND GET AS MANY AS SIX FREE GIFTS...

HOW TO PLAY:

1. With a coin, carefully scratch off the three silver boxes at the right. This makes you eligible to receive one or more free books, and possibly other gifts, depending on what is revealed beneath the scratch-off area.

2. You'll receive brand-new Silhouette Desire® novels, never before published. When you return this card, we'll send you the books and gifts you qualify for *absolutely free*.

3. And, a month later, we'll send you 6 additional novels to read and enjoy. If you decide to keep them, you'll pay only $2.24 per book, a savings of 26¢ per book—plus 69¢ postage and handling per shipment.

4. We'll also send you additional free gifts from time to time, as a token of our appreciation.

5. You must be completely satisfied, or you may return a shipment of books and cancel at any time.

MAKEUP MIRROR AND BRUSH KIT FREE

This lighted makeup mirror and brush kit allows plenty of
light for those quick touch-ups. It operates on two easy-to-
replace bulbs (batteries not included). It holds everything
you need for a perfect finished look yet is small enough to
slip into your purse or pocket—4-1/8″ X 3″ closed. And it
could be YOURS FREE when you play ''LUCKY 7.''

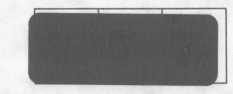

Business Reply Mail

No Postage Stamp Necessary if Mailed in Canada

Postage will be paid by

Silhouette Book Club
P.O. Box 609
Fort Erie, Ontario
L2A 9Z9

Canada Post
Postes Canada
125

DETACH AND MAIL CARD TODAY

"Perfectly," she said succinctly, tilting her own head imperiously.

"Good," he bit back. "Now, is there anything else you have to say before we close this subject?"

Leslie pondered a moment, raking her mind for a suitable retort. Then her green eyes began to gleam and she nodded her head.

"You're great in bed, Falcon," she said wryly, "but you really are an arrogant bastard."

Six

You're great in bed, but you really are a bastard.

A smile relieved the unrelenting line defining Flint's lips. A week and a half had passed since Leslie had made the dry observation, tossing his own words back at him, yet the ghost of a smile haunted his lips every time the echo of her voice teased his memory.

And Leslie wasn't even aware of how fitting her epithet really was! Flint leaned back in his desk chair, his lips curving in a soundless laugh. A week and a half. The reminder of time racing by intruded on his amusement. Leslie had told him that she had planned to spend two weeks in Atlantic City, and now those two weeks were almost past. Unless he could convince her to extend her stay, Leslie would be returning to New York in three days.

The alarm that snaked through Flint both surprised and annoyed him. He had expected to be fully satiated with Leslie long before the end of one week, if not bored to distraction as he always was with any woman. But one week had rushed swiftly into another, and to his chagrin he was neither satiated nor bored. Quite the contrary. Flint could not get enough of Leslie's body or company.

Flint moved as if to shrug off the unusual sensation. He didn't relish feeling any emotion concerning her departure, but most especially he didn't want this uneasy sense of alarm. Flint Falcon considered his life complete—he neither needed nor wanted to form what he considered a crippling emotional dependency on any other individual. Emotional involvements and serious relationships infringed on personal freedom—his personal freedom. And Flint had sworn long ago that nothing would ever again infringe on *his* freedom.

Enthrallment with a woman was not Flint's idea of a fit state to be in; it interfered with a man's work. Frowning, Flint glanced down at the list of postponed appointments lying on his otherwise cleared desktop. He had canceled the appointments the day after he met Leslie simply because his work was infringing on his time with her.

Impatient and disgusted with himself, Flint had requested his secretary to reschedule the appointments. A few minutes later he'd countermanded his own orders, thereby thoroughly confusing the superefficient man, who admired Flint above all others.

Muttering a shocking expletive, Flint spun his chair to face the long expanse of window. The sea and the sky were spread out before him, metaphorically his. It was all Flint needed, or at least it had been all he'd needed until now.

"Dammit!"

Kicking his chair back, Flint sprang to his feet and walked to the window. The bright autumn sunlight danced over the undulating waves like gold coins flung to earth by a benign deity. Overhead, the endless stretch of incredible blue sky was unmarred except for a tiny speck and the wispy line of vapor trailing it. It was freedom. It was his. And yet he felt fettered, caged by the tantalizing personality and sweetly responsive body of a woman!

Flint's brows were inching together in a fierce frown when he heard the faint rustle of movement from the room beyond his office door. Leslie. A sensation too similar to happiness flowed through his entire body. Denying the validity of the sensation, Flint forced himself to remain absolutely still when what he longed to do was stride into the bedroom and sweep Leslie into his arms.

Utter madness! Flint's instinct for self-preservation sent a message of warning to his besotted senses. It was utter madness to allow his emotions to become frazzled over a mere woman.

Ah, but what a woman! Even as his mind rebelled against it, Flint strained to hear the soft sounds of her movements in the bedroom. An image of her swamped his senses and tormented his body. It was three-forty in the afternoon, and he wanted her. His sudden need was nothing new; Flint was getting very familiar with the near-constant state of arousal.

Moving his shoulders in a philosophical shrug, Flint surrendered, savoring the memories they now shared and the anticipation of adding to those memories. There would be time enough to reclaim control of his rioting senses and voracious desire after Leslie was gone, Flint mused confidently.

Only three more days. The phrase stabbed at Flint's mind like a poisoned dart. Moving with sudden decisiveness, he turned his back on the window and headed for the connecting door to the bedroom with long, purposeful strides.

Three days to go.

Catching her lower lip between her teeth, Leslie paused in her restless circuit around the room to stare at the closed door to Flint's office. She felt strange, not at all like the rather cynical woman who'd laughed about indulging in a blazing affair if she should happen to run into a certain type of man.

Well, she *had* literally run into that certain type of man, and being with him was having a strange effect on her mentally and physically. Just the thought of Flint on the other side of the door caused a tingle in her spine and a weakness in her body.

Lord, the man's appetite was insatiable! Her breathing growing rough and uneven, Leslie sank onto the edge of the bed, a mocking smile curving her lips as she recalled her own aggressive behavior in his bed. Falcon's influence on her was astonishing. Never had she taken the initiative while making love. Never had she reveled in playing the wanton. The self-mocking smile deepened as Leslie decided that should the occasion arrive she could now accept the role of Salome, confident of giving an award-winning performance.

Quivering in response to vivid memories, Leslie lay back on the enormous bed. Sighing, she closed her eyes. Flint was consuming her, body and mind, to the extent that he was all she thought about anymore. She wasn't eating well, she wasn't sleeping well; she felt exhausted and exhilarated in turn. And as if her mental and physical state were not enough, thoughts of Flint prevented her from using the casino as an escape hatch—she could no longer *lose* herself in a casino.

If she had believed it at all possible, Leslie might have believed she was falling in love with the enigmatic, confusing man whose bed she so very contentedly shared. But Leslie absolutely refused to so much as entertain the possibility of falling in love with Falcon. In Leslie's oft-stated opinion, love was detrimental to a woman's health and sanity. But she did enjoy being with him, in and out of bed!

Deep in introspection, Leslie didn't hear the office door open, nor did she hear footsteps. Flint's sharp, indrawn breath alerted her to his presence in the bedroom.

"Sleeping again?" his voice was pitched low so as not to disturb her if she had drifted off.

Leslie opened her eyes and caught her breath at the imposing sight he made. He was attired in a three-piece gray suit, but in spite of the conservative clothing, the thought occurred to Leslie that Falcon looked more like a high-priced, cold-eyed hit man than a high-powered executive. Denying that there were times Flint's self-contained aloofness frightened her would have been pointless. Leslie knew instinctively that he possessed the power to hurt just about anyone he wanted to—her most of all. The knowledge instilled wary caution in Leslie.

"I thought you were going to work all afternoon?" she said, recalling his exact words and dismissive tone at breakfast. He'd told her to find her own *amusement* for the day, as he was planning to spend it in his office—which had been declared off limits to her from day one.

Flint didn't respond, at least not verbally. A smile, blatant with sensuality, relieved the severity of his thin lips. His movements precise and economical, he began to undress. One dark eyebrow inched into an arc that silently urged her to follow his lead.

Leslie should have felt anger. She should have felt insulted. She laughed instead and moved to comply with his silent command for participation. "Don't you ever get tired?" she asked, taking her time as she was already partially undressed, having stripped down to bra, panties and a half-slip on her return to the apartment.

Flint paused in the act of removing his shirt to slant a contemplative look at her. His shoulders and chest were exposed, revealing long, hard muscles and a patch of tightly curled black chest hair. Strangely, as Leslie had discovered to her surprise, the rest of Flint's body was smooth and hairless except for a fine, silky down.

"Not often," he said with absolute seriousness. "I have a lot of stamina and staying power."

"I'll say," Leslie muttered, drawing one of his rare barks of laughter from him.

"I work at it," he added, tossing his shirt aside.

"Really?" Leslie frowned. "When?"

Flint stepped out of his slacks and tossed them on top of his shirt before glancing at her. "Every morning, before you're awake." Perching on the side of the bed, he bent to remove his shoes.

Leslie was hard-pressed not to trail her fingers the curved length of his enticing spine. "But how? I mean, where do you work out and what do you do?" she asked, completely forgetting that she was supposed to be undressing.

"I run on the beach every morning." Standing, Flint hooked his thumbs under the elastic waistband on his narrow briefs. "And I swim in the hotel pool," he continued, drawing the briefs over his slim hips and down his taut thighs. As he bent to remove the shorts, his gaze swept her body, which was still clad in bra and panties. "I'm winning this race, Leslie." The shorts landed on top of his piled clothing.

"There's a need for speed?" Leslie asked ingenuously.

"You must not have been paying attention, darling," he drawled, straightening to his full height to reveal the fullness of his arousal, "or you'd know there definitely was a need for speed." Stepping to the bed, he knelt on the mattress beside her and reached around her to unsnap her bra. His warm hands replaced the lace supporting her breasts.

"Flint?" Leslie murmured as he eased her onto her back and covered her with his body.

"Umm?" he murmured, testing the texture of her shoulder with his mouth and tongue.

"I still have my panties on," she whispered, gasping her pleasure as his lips tasted her skin from her shoulder to the tip of one breast.

"I know," he whispered back, aligning his hips with hers as he settled between her silky thighs. "Exciting, isn't it?" he said, closing his lips around the aching crest as he arched his body into hers.

Leslie inhaled sharply, sighing, "Yes!" He was so close, so close, and yet barred from her by a filmy strip of silk. Flint arched again, his body making an urgent demand for entrance. And suddenly, desperately, Leslie wanted his entrance, needed to feel him inside her, filling her emptiness, feeding her hunger. Her trembling fingers fumbled at the wispy bit of nothing.

"Flint," she pleaded when his pressing body impeded her efforts, "please, raise your hips!"

"Not yet." Reaching down, he circled her wrists with his strong fingers, then brought her arms up and over her head. He began to rotate his hips slowly and lowered his head to suckle at her breast.

It was maddening. It was exasperating. It was the most erotic sensation Leslie ever experienced. Within moments she was whimpering low in her throat. Her senses going haywire from the steadily building tension, Leslie helplessly responded to the cadence Flint's motions created. The sensual thread woven through her body tightened to quivering tautness.

"Falcon!" Leslie cried his name as she twisted to free her hands from his firm but gentle clasp.

"Yes, darling?" Flint murmured, caressing her nipple with his tongue one last time before raising his head. Watching the tension mirrored on her face, he continued the rhythmic motion of his hips.

"Let go of my hands! I want to touch you!" she gasped, obeying the dictates of her body and arching to meet his thrust. "Please, Falcon, I want to feel you in—" Leslie's ragged voice rose to a muted scream as the thread of tension snapped, flinging her into a shattering release. "Falcon!"

Flint gentled her with soft words and stroking hands but didn't let the fire go out. With her first unlabored breath, he slipped the panties from her. "And now it gets even more exciting," he whispered, moving between her thighs and entering her body. Slowly at first, then more quickly, his thrusts deeper, he fanned her inner fire into a raging blaze.

Clinging to him, fighting for breath, Leslie was carried along in Flint's flaming tide of passion. She shattered around him again an instant before she felt him explode deep inside her quaking body.

Sunset was spreading its golden mantle over the earth when Leslie came to her senses and felt Flint's hand stroking her inner thigh. Raising her heavy eyelids, she gazed into his eyes.

"I thought you'd fallen asleep again," he murmured, gliding his hand up to possessively cup her breast in his palm.

"No." Leslie smiled and settled her body more firmly against his hand. "I was merely attempting to breathe." Deciding that what was good for the goose, and so forth, she captured him with her fingers; Flint's surprised gasp made the display of boldness worthwhile. But even as she felt the unmistakable stirrings of renewal, Flint moved away from her.

"Later, darling," he promised, bending to her to brush his lips over hers. "But now I'm starving, and you must be also."

"Must I?" Leslie frowned, thinking it odd that she really wasn't at all hungry. "I suppose so," she went on quickly when Flint returned her frown. "But more than food, I really could use a short nap."

Though he sighed, Flint relented. "All right." He brushed his mouth over hers again, then rolled off the bed. "I'll have a snack to hold me until dinner." He stretched lazily, displaying his muscular body for her inspection. "I feel great," he said, grinning down at her. "I think I'll have a swim while you nap." He started for the bathroom, but paused at the door to shoot a stern look at her. "Stop ogling me and get to sleep." His tone was as stern as his expression. "You have one hour, Leslie." Without waiting for either reply or protest from her, Flint strode into the bathroom.

Ogling? Leslie mused sleepily. Had she been ogling his body? Yes, of course she had, she admitted shamelessly. But then, Flint's body deserved female ogling—among other things! Feeling content in body and amused in mind, Leslie yawned, closed her eyes and promptly fell asleep.

For a weeknight, the casino was exceptionally crowded. Standing at a progressive half-dollar machine, Leslie fed her last five coins into it, pulled the handle, then watched as the four reels spun. She shrugged when the reels settled into place, revealing a bar, a blank and two more bars. Turning away, Leslie glanced down at her hands. She had fed the greedy machine five rolls of halves for a single payout of fifty coins, or twenty-five dollars. The luck, or lack of it, didn't bother her, but her coin-blackened fingers did.

Pausing to light a cigarette, Leslie smiled and shook her head at a man who politely asked if she was going to play the machine. Stepping aside, she headed for the ladies' room. Her pace unhurried, she strolled through the casino, her gaze skimming the male faces for a glimpse of Flint, who was somewhere in the large room even though he was not indulging in the games offered.

A soft smile touched her lips as she thought about the seeming contradictions the man presented. She had discovered at the outset that Flint did not gamble, at least not in the casinos. She had also learned early on that although he had a forbidding, unapproachable look about him, Flint was capable of tear-inducing tenderness. And though he projected an image of cold detachment, Flint could generate spine-melting heat with his thoroughly involved lovemaking.

A man of many facets, half of them hidden, Leslie concluded. She sighed with disappointment at not spotting him as she reached her destination. After washing the residue of the coins from her hands, Leslie moved to the long mirror above the vanity countertop. She was brushing clear red color onto her lower lip when two beautiful young women entered the lounge.

"Did you see him?" the one woman, a true blonde, asked the other, a brunette, in a breathless, excited tone.

"Did I see whom?" The brunette responded in a cultured, bored tone.

"The infamous Falcon!" The blonde's awed reply caught the brunette's attention. Suddenly Leslie was very interested as well.

Infamous? Leslie questioned silently, listening closely while appearing to concentrate on outlining her lips.

The brunette's reaction was far from bored. "Flint's here?" she fairly yelped.

Flint? Leslie's eyes narrowed, ostensibly on her makeup.

"Flint?" the blonde repeated, wide-eyed now, her awe obviously doubled. "You know him?"

Good question, Leslie thought, playing deaf as she strained to hear the brunette's answer.

"I've met him." The woman's smile was smug, too smug to suit her unobtrusive eavesdropper.

In bed? Leslie wondered, beginning to simmer as she waited for the query to be asked aloud.

But the blonde's mind was not in the bedroom. "Is it true that he's an ex-con?" she asked in an avidly curious tone.

Leslie nearly dropped the crimson-tipped lipstick brush. Ex-con! Flint? Anger ripped through her. How dare that little fool insinu— "Yes, it's true," the brunette said with absolute certainty. "He served three years of a twenty-year sentence in a prison in New Mexico."

Twenty years! The damning words pounded inside Leslie's head as she collected her makeup and beat a hasty retreat from the room. As the door shut behind her, she sank back against the wall and drew deep gulps of air into her trembling body. What crime had Flint committed to draw a twenty-year sentence? she thought frantically, skipping her wide-eyed gaze over the faces of passersby. Several women, and more men, gazed at her with concern, but only one detached himself from the throng to make his way to her side.

"Are you feeling sick?" Flint's dark brows drew together in a frown as he examined her face.

Leslie stared mutely at his tense expression and slowly shook her head.

"Leslie, what's wrong?" he demanded, grasping her upper arm.

Leslie swallowed. "I—I need a drink." She swallowed again, fighting back a brackish taste. "Can we find someplace to sit down?"

Though Flint's frown deepened, he answered at once. "Of course." Steadying her with his firm grip, he turned and walked with her toward the escalator. "We'll go down to the restaurant." Exasperation overshadowed the concern in his tone. "You barely touched your dinner," he said. "You're probably half-starved."

Food was the last thing on Leslie's mind, but she didn't bother to correct him. Shocked and sick to her stomach, she allowed him to usher her to the restaurant. Since she was no longer surprised by the fact that Flint was apparently recognized by every maître d' in every restaurant in every hotel in Atlantic City, Leslie accepted the effusive attention shown to them by this maître d' as he escorted them to a table. She wasn't even surprised at the relative seclusion afforded by the table; Flint was invariably seated at a secluded table.

Flint took it upon himself to order a sandwich for her when Leslie merely shook her head at the menu the waiter offered her; he ordered wine for the two of them as well. Even though he maintained his intense scrutiny, she kept silent until the waiter departed after delivering their drinks.

"Damn it, Leslie, talk to me," Flint said through gritted teeth when the silence stretched into humming tension between them. "Tell me what is wrong with you."

Leslie moistened her dry throat with a sip of wine. "I, eh, overheard two women talking in the ladies' room," she said, her voice low and reedy.

"So?" Flint demanded.

Lifting her head, she met his narrowed gaze. "They were talking about you."

"So?" he repeated arrogantly. "What did they say?" His gaze held hers.

Leslie inhaled slowly, then threw caution aside—she had to know if what they'd said was true. "The one woman asked the other, who incidentally claimed to know you, whether it was true that you had served time in prison."

Flint stiffened and his expression froze, but his tone was unruffled. "Continue."

Leslie had a terrible feeling of foreboding. "It *is* true, isn't it?" Leslie didn't know quite how she'd expected him to respond, but she certainly hadn't expected him to smile, however faintly.

"Yes, Leslie," he admitted in a cool tone, "it is true."

The feeling of foreboding intensified. "But... why?" she cried in a strangled whisper.

Flint's gaze remained steady. "I was convicted of rape."

Rape! For one instant, Leslie stared at him in horror, her throat closing, her senses whirling. Then her intelligence reasserted itself and her mind called a halt to the dramatics. Rape? she thought, doubt growing. She had shared his bed for almost two weeks; she knew his power and prowess. Flint Falcon need never force himself on any woman!

As Leslie's thinking cleared, so did her vision. His features locked into concealment, Flint was watching her, waiting for her reaction to his words. In actual time, he had waited only seconds.

"I don't believe it." Amazingly, the instant she said the words, all symptoms of shock vanished.

"It's true," he said, still watching her. "I was convicted, and I did serve three years of the sentence."

Leslie shook her head and waved her fingers impatiently as if brushing his admission aside. "I don't believe you ever raped anyone."

"Thank you." Flint's smile brought the color back to her pale cheeks. "And you're right—I never raped anyone, physically or any other way." His head angled into an arrogant tilt. "It's not my style."

"But who accused you of such a terrible thing?" Leslie frowned. Before he could answer, she demanded, "Why would any woman accuse you?"

Flint sat back in his chair, his expression contemplative. It wasn't necessary for him to tell her that he was unused to explaining himself to anybody; Leslie already knew that. Yet, to her astonishment, he proceeded to explain himself to her.

"The woman who accused me was my best friend's...bride." Flint's pause over his last word was telling, as was the sneer that curled his lip. "She did so in an attempt—successful, I might add—to cover her own transgressions." His smile was wry.

Leslie was having enough trouble assimilating the fact that Flint's friend's wife would even dream of accusing him without having to contend with his caginess. She rolled her eyes in exasperation. "You can't let it go at that," she insisted. "Why would she—" Leslie broke off as the waiter arrived with their food. The moment the waiter finished, she moved to push her plate away. Flint's low voice halted her as her fingers touched the plate.

"I'll make a deal with you," he said. "If you'll eat every crumb of that sandwich, I'll try to explain her motives. Deal?" His eyebrows shot into an arch.

"It's a deal," Leslie agreed, picking up half of her sandwich and taking a bite.

Flint favored her with one of his spine-tingling smiles. "Okay, you eat, I'll talk. Don't interrupt." His smile flashed again; Leslie almost choked. "It was all rather stupid," he began in a tone of utter boredom. "As it happened, six months after their wedding, my friend's wife discovered that she was three months pregnant, which in itself should have delighted my friend." He paused for a sip of wine while Leslie took note of the fact that he never referred to his friend by name. When Flint continued speaking, his voice was heavy with cynicism.

"But, understandably, my friend wasn't delighted, since at the time he had supposedly impregnated his wife he was half a world away on special assignment for the oil company that employed him."

"Why, that—" Leslie exclaimed.

"Precisely," Flint concurred, "and you've only heard the half of it. Upon questioning by her outraged husband, the sweet little bride broke down and admitted that she had been raped.''

"He bought that?'' Leslie's expression was skeptical.

Flint laughed sarcastically. "Not initially. But on further questioning the little woman sobbingly named her rapist.''

"You.''

"Yeah.'' Flint sighed the word on a sharp exhale. "He didn't want to believe it, but the evidence, all circumstantial, appeared to give credence to her story. I had been to see her several times during his absence. It was common knowledge to all our friends that I had dated her a couple times before my friend ever met her.'' His lips twisted. "She was very convincing on the stand, weepy and remorseful for being so friendly with me, however innocently.'' He nodded solemnly. "She gave a great performance. The jury was out less than twenty minutes.'' He sneered. "And twenty was the magic word; they gave me twenty years.''

"Oh, Flint.'' Leslie's lips were dry, but her eyes were wet.

Flint shook his head. "It's over and not worth your tears.''

Leslie took a sip of her wine and dashed her tears away with her fingers. "You were paroled?''

"I was exonerated.'' His smile held a tinge of pity. "I had served three years of the sentence when my friend caught his wife with another man. He finally forced the truth out of her; then he took her to repeat her story to the authorities.'' He shrugged. "And here I am—'' he inclined his head toward her plate "—waiting for you to finish that sandwich.''

Leslie obediently lifted the second half of her sandwich. "Didn't your friend ever try to contact you?" she asked, immediately biting into the sandwich.

"He tried," Flint drawled.

"You wouldn't see him?"

"What do you think?"

"I think you're very hard."

This time, Flint's laughter held a biting tone. "With reason, darling, with reason."

"I know." She sighed. "But even though he should have believed you," she argued, wondering why she was playing the devil's advocate, "he loved her, Flint. She betrayed both of you."

"Love." Flint snorted. "If that's what love does to a man's brains, I'll take a rain check, thank you. And anyway, why are you pleading for love? It sure as hell gave you nothing but grief."

"Too true." Conceding the point with a smile but wondering why she felt suddenly empty, Leslie polished off her food and wine, then tossed her napkin onto the table. She needed people, faceless people, and action, gaming action. In short, Leslie suddenly needed her escape hatch. Flipping her mane back with one hand, she gave him her most rakish grin.

"I feel wonderful now that I've eaten," she lied. "And now I want to play until they toss me out at closing time."

Seven

It didn't work anymore, dammit! It simply didn't work, Leslie thought, staring disinterestedly at the cards before her on the table. She had been sitting at the blackjack table for nearly two hours. She had even won a tidy sum of money. And she was bored, bored, bored!

Dejected, Leslie fingered two ten-dollar chips, responding automatically to the table play. And the evening had begun with such promise, too, she reflected, suppressing a sigh.

Flint had allowed her to sleep a half hour over his deadline, and when he had woken her it had been with light kisses and teasing admonitions to "Get it in gear, woman."

He had set the mood, and Leslie had happily gone along with him. The bantering and teasing had continued while they dressed and through dinner. Though Flint's accusation about her barely touching her meal was correct, Leslie had thoroughly enjoyed herself, laughing discreetly at his droll yet on-target observations concerning the various modes of dress displayed by the other patrons in the restaurant.

From the restaurant they had gone on to a show at the theater in Falcon's Flight, becoming one with the rest of the audience in their enjoyment of an outrageously funny young comedian who had preceded an aging singer on the program. Still in high spirits, they had left after the show to prowl the casinos. The downhill slide for Leslie had begun when those two women had entered the ladies' room.

"Dealer pays nineteen."

Leslie blinked and stared at her cards, an eight, a deuce and an ace. It was time to quit. She didn't even remember signaling for an additional card! Watching the dealer stack her winning chips into a neat pile, Leslie crushed out the cigarette she couldn't recall lighting, let alone smoking. Yes, she decided, motioning to the dealer that she was out of the play, it was definitely time to quit.

Scooping the chips into her beaded black silk evening bag, Leslie smiled at the dealer and turned away from the table. Flint found her at the exchange desk just as the attendant was counting out crisp new bills to the tune of seven hundred dollars.

"Hey, beautiful," he murmured close to her ear. "Since you got lucky, want to hire my services for what's left of the night?"

With a mercurial switch, Leslie's spirits soared again. Laughing, she glanced at the desk attendant. If

the young man had overheard Flint's suggestion, he
hid his reaction well behind a bland expression. Stuff-
ing the bills into her purse, she turned to face Flint.
His eyebrows were raised slightly, as if in expectation
of a reply from her.

Leslie ran a contemplative glance the length of his
lean, gorgeous body. "Are you any good?" she asked
haughtily.

"No." Flint grinned wickedly. "I'm very bad."

"Are you very expensive?" Leslie purred.

"No." Flint's eyes glittered with devilry. "But I'm
very demanding."

Leslie gave him a slow smile and a smoldering look
from her long, shimmering green eyes. "Sold," she
said in a throaty voice, linking her arm through his.
"Your place or your place?"

"You're really ready to leave?" Flint attempted an
expression of amazement. "A full forty-five minutes
before closing time?"

"I'm really ready to leave," Leslie said, mimicking
his tone. "A full forty-five minutes before closing
time." She paused for effect. "If you will be so kind
as to retrieve my stole from coatcheck?"

"Done," he said, striding away from her. "I'll meet
you at the front entrance."

"No! Flint, the boardwalk entrance!" Leslie called
after him. Flint pivoted to stare at her.

"You want to walk at this hour of the morning?"

"I like to walk." Leslie shrugged. "Besides, I need
some fresh air. Okay?"

Flint smiled. "Whatever. A brisk walk in the cold
air always stimulates my, er, appetite."

The air was cold. Leslie stood still on the board-walk, inhaling the scent of the sea. "Umm," she murmured, smiling up at Flint. "I love the seashore; the atmosphere, the smell, even the noisy seabirds. But most of all I love the sense of peace and freedom I al-ways feel by just gazing at the restless ocean."

"I know what you mean." Flint had shifted his gaze to stare out at the inky, white-capped waves. "For all its power, the sea instills a strange sense of serenity on its observers."

They were silent for long moments, each into their own thoughts, drinking in the night and the Atlan-tic's ambience. Leslie shivered, breaking the quiet.

"You're cold," Flint said briskly, draping his left arm around her shoulders to draw her close to the warmth of his body. "Come on, woman, let's go home to bed."

"You know, Falcon, you really are a self-confident so-and-so," she said, laughing and curling her arm around his waist and snuggling close to him as she fell into step with him.

Flint didn't answer, but without breaking stride he bent to capture her mouth with his own. Oblivious to everything but each other, neither Leslie nor Flint no-ticed the shadow that detached itself from the depths of an entranceway to a closed, dark store. The first sign of danger came with the sound of a low, raspy male voice.

"How romantic," the voice sneered. "If you want to live to get what all this kissin' is leading up to, man, hand over your wallet and don't play the hero."

Leslie's feet froze to the boardwalk as her glance sliced to the barely discernible figure of the young, scraggly-looking man crowding Flint's right side. The man was dressed in jeans and a poplin windbreaker with slash side pockets. He had his right hand inside the jacket pocket, and Leslie's horrified eyes saw the outline of what appeared to be a gun pressing against the material. His face was shadowed by the brim of the cap he'd pulled low over his forehead. Moonlight reflected glints of gold off a small hoop looped through his pierced ear.

Flint didn't say a word, nor did he seem to move as much as a muscle. Seconds passed; then, with blurring swiftness, Flint went into action. Suddenly his right hand was level with the startled man's jaw, and the moonlight reflected off the gleaming steel blade that was held almost casually in his fingers. Flint flexed his wrist and the blade speared the man's earring, gold encircling steel.

The thief gave a muffled yelp as Flint's wrist flexed again and the blade moved, tearing the ring from his ear. Leslie watched as the gold hoop spiraled into the air before plunging to earth. The would-be attacker was babbling before the ring landed on the boards.

"Hey, man, don't cut me!" he gasped, shrinking back as Flint moved the tip of the blade from the man's ear to his jugular vein. Though the point of the blade made an indentation in the skin, it didn't draw blood.

"*Man* is the operative word, *boy*." Flint's voice was low and contained an iciness that chilled Leslie's spine. "Let me offer you some free advice," he added in that same icy tone. "Don't horse around with a half-breed with a knife up his sleeve."

The young man was gasping for breath when two tall shapes materialized to stand on either side of Flint.

"You all right, Mr. Falcon?"

What little breath Leslie had left in her body swished out in relief as she recognized Flint's bodyguards. In a blink the blade was gone, back to its home nestled close to Flint's arm.

"Yeah," Flint muttered, tightening his hold on Leslie's shoulders as he began to move away. "Take care of this two-bit amateur."

"Yes, sir!" the guard called to Flint's back.

Leslie was cold, so very cold, frozen to the depths of her being. The incident had frightened her badly; Falcon had frightened her even more. Flint hadn't been frightened—that Leslie knew without a doubt. Flint hadn't appeared to feel much of anything except an icy anger. A shudder ripped through Leslie's already trembling body. Flint's arm tightened on her.

"Damned punk." Flint's coldly snarled curse intensified the chill permeating Leslie. "It's over, Leslie. Forget it." His cool attitude dismissed the attack as if it had been of little importance.

Forget it! She screamed silently. She'd never forget it! And she'd never forget the glimpse she'd had of *him*—the inner him. The man he had revealed to her within those brief seconds was cold, unfeeling, incapable of human fear and emotion! Leslie's thoughts tumbled wildly. Flint Falcon really was like a devil incarnate, inhuman! Leslie shivered visibly.

The warmth inside Flint's apartment had no effect on the chill gripping Leslie. His gaze narrowed on her white, pinched face. Flint released her only long

enough to secure the lock; then he drew her back into
a close embrace.

"Leslie, relax," he murmured into her hair. "You're
safe here."

Leslie bit back hysterical laughter. Safe? Oh, God!
Closing her eyes, she willed herself into utilizing her
acting talent. "I'm sorry, but nothing like that has ever
happened to me before. I—I know it happens all the
time," she babbled on, unable to stop herself. "Not
only here in Atlantic City but in cities large and small
all over the world. It's just that it has never happened
to *me*!"

Flint's broad hand stroked her quivering back.
"Actually, you were not in any real danger at any
time," he said softly. "To get at you, he would have
had to go through me."

The arrogant self-confidence underlining his soft
voice snapped the last of Leslie's control. Afraid she'd
literally fall apart, she pushed herself away from him.
"I'm, uh, going to take a hot shower," she blurted out
when he frowned. "Maybe it will take away the chill,
at least on the outside." Scooping the velvet robe from
the foot of the bed, she dashed for the bathroom.

"I'll have a brandy waiting for you," Flint called
after her, "to take the chill from the inside."

A brandy? *A* brandy? Leslie repeated to herself as
the hot water burst from the shower to cascade over
her body. She was afraid that an entire cask of brandy
could not take the chill from inside her body.

But the shower did help, as did the brandy. Calmer,
in control again, Leslie sipped the last of the fiery liquid. Avoiding Flint's intent stare, she set the glass aside
and stood up.

"Better?" Flint asked in a strained, unnatural voice.

"Yes, thank you," Leslie responded politely, like a well-mannered child. "I think I'll go to bed now." She was slipping from the robe when she heard his murmured reply.

"Yes, I think we will."

They lay side by side on the enormous bed, not sleeping, not speaking, not touching. Eyes wide as she stared at the white ceiling, Leslie fought against the conflicting emotions tearing her in different directions. One part of her wanted to escape from this man devoid of emotion, to run as fast as she could to the safety of New York, her own apartment, her friends. Another part of her longed to turn to Flint, to curl her body close to his, to feel again the sheer joy of his kiss, his touch, his possession. When he spoke suddenly, the harsh sound of his voice made her flinch.

"It's made a difference, hasn't it? It's turned you off."

"What?" Turning her head on the pillow to face him, Leslie frowned in confusion at the tight set of his features. "What are you talking about?" She was positive he had read her reaction to the cold, deadly man he'd revealed to her, but she was wrong.

"Knowing I'm a half-breed has made a difference, hasn't it?" he demanded through gritted teeth. "You no longer want me touching you."

"That's not true!" Leslie denied indignantly. "I never gave it a second thought!" she said truthfully.

"Prove it," Flint taunted.

"How?" she cried. "What can I say to—"

"Kiss me, caress this body that contains the mixture of blood from a white man and a Navaho woman."

"Oh, Flint," Leslie sighed, feeling the pain hidden beneath his rough tone; perhaps he was capable of some emotion after all.

"Do it!" he ordered harshly.

Since it was what she'd been aching to do anyway, Leslie obeyed him, turning her body against his to seek his mouth with her trembling lips. Flint was not easily convinced, but Leslie fully enjoyed the task of erasing his doubt. Slow kisses and gentle caresses eased away the conflict inside Leslie and the constraint between her and Flint. Their loveplay was just heating up when Flint crushed her breasts with his chest and stared at her with eyes that glittered wickedly.

"Shall I play the savage for you?" One dark eyebrow arched questioningly.

"What?" Leslie said, laughing and shaking her head in confusion.

"I asked if you'd like me to play the savage for you," Flint repeated. "Most women love it. Perhaps you would, too."

Leslie could barely breathe with the pressure from his chest, yet she managed to raise her voice slightly in exasperation. "Flint, please ease up a little—you're crushing me!" When he propped himself up on his forearms, she sighed her relief. "Thank you. Now will you explain what the hell you've been talking about? And don't categorize me with most women!"

Flint's lips twitched in amusement for a moment, but flattened when he began to speak. "When I was in my junior year of college, an eastern college, the word spread that I was a half-breed. And though I had never had difficulty finding a date, suddenly I was one very popular *brave* with the ladies.'' The contempt in his tone caused a shaft of pain in Leslie's chest. "Being a fairly bright boy, it didn't take me long to figure out that, titillated by the books they'd read and movies they'd seen, the girls were panting to be ravaged by the savage.''

"And you were happy to accommodate them,'' Leslie said dryly.

"I never was stupid,'' Flint retaliated every bit as dryly. "But I was selective even then,'' he drawled.

"And did you learn to ravage like a savage?'' Leslie inquired blandly.

"Oh, yes, I learned,'' he retorted. "They taught me.''

"How?'' she asked, already certain she knew the answer.

"Those sweet, innocent, giggling coeds whipped this savage into shape by biting and kicking and clawing bloody ridges into my back. And do you know what I've learned since then?''

Leslie bit her lip and shook her head.

"Those college girls have grown-up sisters all over the place, my friend's bride included.''

"Flint, you didn't—'' she began.

"You're damned right I didn't,'' he interrupted. "But it wasn't from lack of effort on her part. He had asked me to look after her for him, and the first time I stopped by to see how she was doing, she was after me.'' Flint's curling lip revealed hard white teeth. "She actually begged me. She wasn't the first.'' His contempt was palpable in the space between them. "She wasn't the last, either."

Leslie drew herself together, her spine so rigid it quivered. "And now you expect me to beg like they did?" Cold rejection coated her tone.

"No, Leslie." Flint smiled sensuously. "But I was hoping you'd want to see the savage."

"Oh, but you're not a savage, Mr. Falcon, remember?" Leslie reminded him nicely. "You are a bastard."

Laughing, Flint lowered his head to hers; then he was laughing into her mouth. "You have my permission to bite me and kick me and even claw me all you want," he growled. "But only in response to the passion *I* arouse in you."

"I won't!" Leslie gasped, thrilling to the fire his touch sent crackling through her body. But, to her own abashed amazement, she did.

Flint was rarely out of Leslie's sight during the last two days of her vacation. In truth, he was rarely out of the bed. Yet regardless of how often, how completely he possessed her, he couldn't seem to get enough, and his lovemaking grew steadily more intense, almost desperate.

As she was beginning to feel somewhat desperate herself, Leslie matched his urgency. And when they occasionally did desert the apartment to go out for dinner or visit the casinos, she was restless and depressed until they returned.

The situation alarmed Leslie. With each passing hour, each passing minute, Flint was becoming more important to her. The realization of how much he was beginning to mean to her scared her witless. She was going to be hurt very badly, and she knew it. She had recognized and identified his character. Flint was a law unto himself—arrogant, competent, self-confident, sublimely male and serenely alone. Though he felt passion, he was cold. Though he could show tenderness, he was detached. Though he could make love, he was immune to the emotion.

After two weeks in his company, Leslie had reached the disheartening conclusion that Flint Falcon merely tolerated women. His experiences with women had left him bitter and cynical. Knowing just a small bit of his history, Leslie both understood and despaired over his attitude.

Leslie felt that if she didn't get out of his life as fast as her car could take her she would literally wind up begging him to... What? Leslie closed her mind to contemplation of this crucial question.

On the morning she had originally planned on leaving, Leslie stood in the bedroom, suitcase open on the bed, skimming her gaze over the room to double-check if she had missed anything. Her gaze came to rest on the window, and a soft sigh whispered through her lips. She'd had the blazing affair she had laughingly promised herself—only now she wasn't laughing.

The morning sunshine sparkled off the window, dazzling her eyes. Telling herself the light was too bright, Leslie blinked against a tide of warm moisture and glanced away.

How does one say goodbye to a lover? she wondered, swallowing hard to ease the tightness in her throat. She was such a novice at this most intimate of games, and considering how devastated she was feeling, Leslie was positive she would remain a novice. She felt slightly sick and tight inside, and she wanted to fling herself onto the bed and weep. But more than anything else she wanted to stay with Flint. Leslie shivered when the sound of his voice followed her thought.

"You could wait to leave until later this afternoon," Flint suggested softly from directly behind her.

Fighting an overwhelming temptation to turn and fling herself into his arms, Leslie clenched her teeth and shook her head. "No. I want to avoid the worst of the traffic." She shut her eyes and bit her lip when his arms encircled her waist.

"And I want you," he murmured, turning her to face him. "One more time." His narrowed eyes swept to her mouth as he slowly lowered his head.

"There's no time!" Leslie protested, terrified that if he kissed her she'd disgrace herself by begging him to let her stay.

"There's always time," he argued.

Flint's kiss was hot and hard and fiercely possessive. His hands were sure and swift. Within minutes her suitcase was in a corner, the tailored slacks and silk shirt, which had been smooth and neat moments before, lay in a rumpled heap on the floor, and she lay naked beneath him on the bed.

Furious with him and herself and aroused beyond bearing, Leslie glared up at him. "You don't even like women," she accused on a hissed breath.

For an instant, Flint looked startled. Then he smiled. "I've acquired a taste for redheads," he teased.

"There are dozens of redheads in this city," she retorted.

"But I've acquired a taste for redheaded actresses." He laughed.

"There are hundreds of redheaded actresses in the world," she snapped, needing him and hating herself for her need.

"But I want one particular redheaded actress," he murmured, bringing his mouth to hers.

Leslie returned his kiss, as she had known all along that she would. And even as her hand restlessly skimmed his body as if to impress the feel of him into her skin, Flint drew back to examine every inch of her as if to imprint the sight of her on his memory. His lips followed the passage his burning gaze had mapped out.

"Leslie, Leslie," he groaned, crushing her mouth as he thrust into her arching body. "Kiss me, touch me, lo—" His words were lost in the depths of her throat, and Leslie heard nothing more than the muffled sound of his voice calling her name.

Leslie was exhausted. A half sigh, half sob of relief shuddered through her lips as she drove the car into the Lincoln Tunnel. The city traffic was a mess, as it was every day at five-fifteen. She was so tired, so very tired. Brushing tears from her eyes, Leslie missed the light as it turned green and had to endure the blast of a car horn and an obscene shout from the driver behind her.

Leslie, Leslie.

The echo of Flint's voice hammered in her aching head. Leslie's lips twisted cynically. How quickly the sound of his voice had changed once he'd attained satisfaction.

Flint had left the bed immediately after his breathing had returned to normal. Ignoring his clothing, he strode from the room, leaving the bathroom for her. Feeling of no more importance to him than his discarded clothes, Leslie crawled from the bed to the shower.

But the woman who faced Flint when he strode back into the bedroom thirty minutes later let none of her pain show. Leslie had the regal look of a queen. Her back straight, her head held high, her red hair draping her shoulders like a mantilla of flame, Leslie played out the most exacting performance of her life. Inside she felt as if some part of her was dying, and she prayed Flint's cool, piercing gaze would not penetrate the thin veneer of her act.

"I've sent the bags down," she said coolly, indicating the absence of her cases with a graceful sweep of her hand. "And I've asked for the car to be brought to the entrance."

"I'd have done that," Flint replied tersely.

"Not necessary," she said, shrugging. "It's time I left." Grabbing her coat from where she'd placed it over the back of a chair, she walked to the door.

Flint stopped her as she grasped the doorknob. "No farewell kiss, Leslie?"

"I assumed you had said your farewell on the bed, Falcon," she gibed, keeping herself composed by sheer willpower.

"Just one more kiss," he murmured into her hair. "A kiss between friends."

"Are we friends?" Leslie turned to stare at him.

"Of course." Flint's remote tone and faint smile hurt her heart.

Affecting an equal remoteness, Leslie raised her head, offering her closed mouth to him. His kiss was impersonal, almost chaste, and very nearly destroyed her. Ignoring her protests, Flint escorted her to her car and held the door while she slipped under the steering wheel.

"Goodbye, Falcon," she said as he closed her in and himself out.

"I'll call you sometime, friend." Flint's tone was remote, and to Leslie's ears dismissive.

Though she stiffened, she managed to drive away smoothly from the hotel. A mixture of anger and humiliation sustained her throughout the long drive back to New York.

I'll call you sometime, friend.

He forgot to add: *but don't hold your breath*, Leslie thought. She grimaced as she missed the curb by a hair when she turned into the garage where she kept her car. Leslie allowed herself no illusions. She had served her purpose, and now her usefulness to him was history. She had been dismissed. Flint would not call.

Home. Closing her apartment door a short time later, Leslie glanced around vaguely. It seemed as if she'd been away a very long while. What was home, she wondered, trailing listlessly into her bedroom. A few walls, a collection of furnishings, a telephone listed under her name? Home was supposed to be love and warmth and shared memories and laughter. She had no home. She had a career.

She was so tired. Dropping her suitcases to the floor, Leslie undressed and slid into bed. She wouldn't think, she wouldn't feel, she'd rest and forget him, she assured herself bracingly. Then, curling into a tight ball, Leslie sobbed her misery into the pillow.

Eight

—

You look ghastly, worse than before you left for Atlantic City."

"Thanks." Leslie gave Marie a wry look and took a deep draw on her cigarette. "It's nice to know that I can depend on my friends to tell me the truth." She grimaced. The truth was she felt even worse than she looked.

"Well, it is the truth, Leslie, and I'm worried about you!" Marie frowned and peered into Leslie's face. "You have dark circles under your eyes, your color's bad and you've lost weight," she said, enumerating the points of concern. "I thought the whole idea of a vacation was to relax, but you're in worse shape now than while you were going through the divorce." Marie paused for breath, but she wasn't finished. "You're not eating, and you're smoking like a forest fire."

Reaching across the kitchen table, she grasped Leslie's hand. "You're my best friend, and I'm seriously worried. Won't you tell me what's bothering you?"

Leslie's throat tightened, and tears rushed to fill her eyes at her friend's obvious concern for her. Every word Marie had spoken was true. Leslie was aware of how she looked and how she felt, and that was, in a word, rotten. She felt sleepy all the time, yet she was sleeping badly. She was excessively tired. Her body ached. She was depressed. And her throat had felt scratchy since right after she'd returned from Atlantic City. She was a mess and she knew it. But talking about it . . .

"Is it money?" Marie asked softly when Leslie failed to respond. "Are you in financial trouble?"

Leslie's smile was wan. How very characteristic of Marie to think of money as the cause of her problem, Leslie reflected, dredging up a faint but genuine smile. "No, Marie." She shook her head and winced against a twinge of pain in her throat. "I don't need money."

"But then what is it?" Marie exclaimed. Her eyes widened with anxiety. "Are you ill?"

"No." Leslie started to shake her head again but, mindful of the pain, halted the motion. A frown creased her smooth brow. "At least I don't think so," she amended. "I have been bothered by a persistent sore throat," she admitted.

The maternal instincts in Marie rose to the fore. "Have you seen a doctor?" she demanded, jumping up and skirting the table to place her palm on Leslie's forehead.

"No, Marie, I . . ."

"I know—" Marie made a face "—you don't like doctors." Her eyes narrowed. "I think you have a fever."

"Marie…" Leslie tried unsuccessfully to get a word in. Turning away, Marie hurried from the kitchen.

"I'll get the aspirin."

Leslie sighed with acceptance as Marie's voice floated back to her from the other room. Moments later, Marie came rushing back, a small bottle in her hands.

"Thank heavens little Tony finally fell asleep," she mumbled, shaking two pills into her palm. "And big Tony's glued to the game on the tube." Stepping to the sink, she filled a glass with water, then turned, proffering both glass and pills to Leslie. "You take these," she ordered briskly. "Then you and I are going to have a long talk."

Knowing it would be useless to argue, Leslie obediently swallowed the aspirin, wincing as the pills scraped her tender throat on the way down. Only with Marie, Leslie thought with amusement, could she be invited to dinner and wind up receiving medical attention. Her lips curved into an affectionate smile as she returned the glass to Marie's waiting hand. "Thank you."

"You're welcome." Marie smiled back. "Could you handle some more wine, or would you like something else? A cup of tea, maybe?" she added before Leslie had a chance to respond.

"Marie, you know I detest tea!" Leslie chided in a dry croak. "But I'd love another glass of wine—if it's not Tony's last bottle?" Her eyebrows rose questioningly.

Marie favored her with what Leslie had always secretly thought of as *the look* and waved her hand dismissively. "It isn't his last bottle, but even if it were it wouldn't matter." She retrieved the wine from a bottle rack inside the refrigerator and two stemmed glasses from a cabinet. "Come on," she said, heading for the doorway. "Let's get comfortable."

"But what about the dinner dishes?"

Marie shrugged. "I'll clean that mess up later. It's not going anywhere."

Leslie stared at her in astonishment. Marie must really be concerned if she was prepared to walk away from a cluttered kitchen, Leslie marveled. Marie was the most fastidious housekeeper Leslie had ever known. Her throat growing thick with emotion again, Leslie meekly followed the other woman into the small, neat living room.

"Okay, let's hear it," Marie said in a no-nonsense tone as Leslie settled into a chair opposite her own. "And don't even try telling me it's all from your sore throat, because I won't buy it." Marie's face was stern. "Something's tearing you apart inside, and it shows."

Feeling foolish and very uncertain, Leslie stared into the pale gold wine shimmering in the delicate glass Marie handed to her. She hated the way she was feeling, but she hated the reason for the way she was feeling even more. Mooning like a lovesick fictional heroine over a man, any man, was playing hell with the image of an independent, self-sufficient, mature woman Leslie had worked so hard to create.

"Leslie!" Marie wailed. "You confided in me during that dreadful period with Brad. Why can't you talk to me now?'' Marie's soft brown eyes held a wounded look.

"This is different," Leslie muttered. "This was my own fault."

"What was your own fault?" Marie cried in exasperation.

Leslie played for time by taking a long swallow of wine. Then, assured by Marie's bulldog expression that she wasn't about to give up the subject, Leslie sighed in defeat.

"Do you remember what I said to you before I left for Atlantic City?" she asked in a strained voice.

Marie frowned; then her eyes widened. She nodded once, as if confirming her own thoughts. "You met a man," she stated.

"Yes, I met a man." Leslie's sigh held the sound of utter weariness. Marie was quiet a moment; then her eyes widened even more.

"You really had an affair?" she gasped in disbelief.

"Yes." The husky sound of Leslie's voice could not be blamed entirely on her sore throat. "I—I met him mere moments after I arrived at the Falcon's Flight hotel."

"But..." Marie shook her head as if to clear her mind. "Who is he?"

Leslie took another, longer swallow of wine, then sighed. "His name is Flint Falcon. He owns the hotel."

"You had an affair with Flint Falcon!" Marie nearly shouted. Her extraordinary reaction brought a frown to Leslie's brow.

"You've heard of him?"

"Well, certainly. Who hasn't?" Marie groaned and rolled her eyes. "You mean you hadn't heard of him—before you met him, I mean?"

"No." Leslie's frown deepened. "How could I have?"

Marie gave her a long-suffering look. "You could read a newspaper now and then or catch the news on TV, you know."

"Flint has been written up in the papers?" Leslie asked faintly.

"And been covered thoroughly on the tube," Marie retorted.

Positive the coverage had been about his incarceration for rape, Leslie felt suddenly sick. Hadn't Flint had to bear enough by being imprisoned for a crime he didn't commit, she thought angrily, without having his name dragged through every tabloid as well? Absently picking at the upholstery on the chair arm with her restless fingers, Leslie looked directly at Marie. "What did they say about him?"

"Nothing very good." Marie grimaced. "Since it was some months back, while the hotel was under construction, I don't remember all of it."

"The coverage was about the hotel?" Leslie asked hopefully, shuddering with relief when Marie nodded vaguely.

"It was one of those character studies of the movers and the shakers." When Leslie nodded but remained silent, Marie continued. "The character that emerged of Flint Falcon was not very appealing, and I can't imagine how you of all people could have gotten involved with him."

"He's—er—Flint's very compelling," Leslie muttered.

"And if the stories are to be believed," Marie said, "Falcon is cold, calculating, unemotional, shrewd and single-minded in his drive to succeed." Her expression turned pensive. "It seems that somehow, nobody knows quite how, he managed to gather enough capital over the last five years to either buy or build a number of casinos and casino hotels. Falcon's Flight is, if memory serves, his fourth." Marie paused for breath before adding, "He also is reputed to be hell on wheels with the ladies." She raised her eyebrows pointedly.

Leslie got the point; in fact, it stuck in her most vulnerable spot. She longed to deny every word Marie had spoken against Flint, but in all honesty could not. Hadn't she accused him of the same characteristics? Leslie knew she had, yet she burned with the desire to defend Flint to her friend.

"He's—Flint's not a bad person," she said, her eyes showing life for the first time in weeks.

Marie looked less than impressed. "He seems to have done a real number on you," she observed, scrutinizing Leslie's flushed face. "I'd like to give a piece of my mind to the son of a—" Marie bit the word back; she never swore.

"Flint is not to blame!" Leslie protested harshly. "I walked into the affair with my eyes wide open."

"Oh, Leslie." Sighing heavily, Marie shook her head. "You sure have a lousy talent for picking men."

Leslie took the opportunity to change the subject. "But I do have a talent for picking the right acting roles," she said, albeit somewhat wryly. "And I've

just read a script with a female lead that has me sali-
vating to perform it.''

"You're thinking of going back to work already?''
Marie's face was a study in consternation.

"I am going back to work,'' Leslie corrected her.
"I've agreed to do the play. My agent is closing the
deal.''

"Instead of going to work, you should be consulting a doctor,'' Marie chided her. Leslie's jaw firmed.

"I'm going back to work.''

Before that week was out, Leslie discovered that it
was one thing to say that she was going back to work
and quite another to do it. She felt worse with each
passing day. Her throat was inflamed, her glands were
swollen, her body ached and, regardless of how many
hours she spent asleep, she felt fatigued. She was also
becoming more depressed and teary-eyed with each
successive day. As Leslie had reached the conclusion
that depression and tears produced nothing but tat-
tered emotions and a ravaged appearance, she had
scrupulously avoided indulgence in either since she'd
put herself together after her divorce. Yet each successive day found her more deeply depressed and more
teary-eyed. Near the end of that week, Leslie gave up
and made an appointment with her physician.

The doctor took Leslie to task for waiting so long
before coming to see him, examined her and then told
her he wanted to do some blood tests. Until the test
results were ready, Leslie was ordered to stay as inac-
tive as possible. When the results were in, Leslie sighed
and accepted the fact that she would not be going back
to work for some time. The tests were conclusive.

Somehow, somewhere, Leslie had contracted mononucleosis.

The casino hummed with the muted roar of wall-to-
wall humanity.

Standing unobtrusively against one dull black support pillar, Flint surveyed the area through dispas-
sionate, narrowed eyes. Business was more than good;
it was excellent. Both the hotel and casino had been
packed with eager patrons every day since the opening five weeks earlier. Though pleased by the initial
success of his venture, Flint felt none of the bone-deep
satisfaction he should have been experiencing.

A light began blinking and a bell ringing on a dollar machine in the aisle to Flint's left. His face impas-
sive, Flint glanced at the couple in front of the
machine. They were laughing and exchanging looks,
and the dollar tokens were clanging into the catch tray.
Something about the scene sparked a memory in Flint,
and a smile softened his tight lips.

Leslie had hit that same type of payoff on the night
of her arrival in Atlantic City. Suddenly Flint could see
her face, hear her voice, smell her particular scent as
if she was standing beside him. The sensation was
growing familiar to him. Flint no longer looked
around for her, his heart kicking into a joyous beat.

Pushing away from the support, Flint strolled
through the huge casino, nodding to pit bosses and
floor managers, oblivious now to the sound and press
of people in pursuit of gambling pleasure. He walked
directly to the private elevator.

As usual when entering the apartment, Flint paused
on the wide landing; lately, though, his glance did not

lift automatically to the window wall. His eyes dark and brooding, Flint surveyed the place, compelled by a force he couldn't control. She was not there; he knew she was not there. Still, he searched for her.

He stood on the landing mere seconds, yet the pause was telling. Suppressing a sigh containing elements Flint was unwilling to examine, he walked to the curving staircase and mounted the stairs, heading for his office.

The stack of newspapers, national and international, lay on his desk as they did every afternoon. Ignoring the expanse of window, Flint dropped into his chair and picked up the paper on top of the pile. Quickly reading the articles that interested him and skimming the rest, Flint worked his way through the news, as he did each and every day.

He was over halfway through the pile when he clutched the paper, making it crackle. The paper was a New York daily. The name Leslie Fairfield had seemed to jump out at him from midway into a gossip column. His features rigid, Flint carefully read the three-sentence tidbit of information:

Sorry to hear that the incomparable Leslie Fairfield has had to withdraw from the cast of new play *Crossroads* because of illness. Get well and come back soon, Ms. Fairfield. Broadway misses you.

Because of illness. Flint read the three words again and again. Leslie was ill? A feeling too similar to panic to be tolerated froze his mind. Leslie was ill! Tossing the paper aside, Flint snatched up the phone. He had to talk to her, find out what was... No! Flint shook his head decisively. He had to see her.

Pressing the disconnect button to cancel the long-distance number, Flint then stabbed his finger on the button that would connect him with the phone in his secretary's office on the floor below.

Less than an hour later, Flint strode through the plate-glass doors at the hotel entrance and across the rain-spattered pavement to the black stretch limousine waiting with motor purring at the curb.

The sound of rain dancing against the windowpane was supposed to be soothing, Leslie thought, sighing as her gaze followed one wet runnel to the outside sill. But she didn't feel soothed. She felt restless and moody and... Leslie sighed again. She was missing Flint, more, much more than she ever would have believed it possible to miss any one person.

What was he doing, she wondered, staring sight-lessly at the gray sky beyond her bedroom window. Did he ever miss her? Leslie's lips twisted at the sharp pain that gripped her chest. Of course he wasn't missing her, she chided herself scathingly. If Flint had missed her he'd have called, as he had said he would. Flint hadn't called, hadn't attempted to contact her in any way. Flint had had the affair he'd wanted, and he'd obviously enjoyed their two weeks of pleasurable self-indulgence. But by his remote withdrawal on the morning she'd left the hotel he had also made it obvious that their association was over.

Tears rushed to sting Leslie's eyes, and flinging the covers back impatiently she dragged her tired body from the bed. Dammit, she hated this! She railed si-

lently, reaching for the emerald velvet robe lying across
the foot of the bed. She hated the illness debilitating
her body; she hated the depression and tendency to
tears inherent in the infection. She hated being confined to her apartment with precious little company
but her own self-pitying thoughts. She hated Flint
Falcon. And she hated this damned robe!

Her actions contradicting her raging thoughts, Leslie clutched the garment to her breasts and rubbed her
cheek against the soft velvet nap. No, she amended,
sniffing. She didn't hate the robe, she loved it. As she
loved the man who had purchased it simply because it
had reminded him of her eyes. And Leslie knew that
it was because she loved Flint Falcon so completely
that she at times hated him.

Shivering, Leslie pulled the robe on as she trailed
listlessly into the living room. A half hour later, she
was exhausted but still wandering from room to room,
too restless to sit for more than a few seconds in any
one place.

Leslie was standing at the living room window,
scarcely aware of the increasing intensity of the rain,
when a key was turned in the lock on her apartment
door and Marie stepped into the room. A look of astonishment spread over her face as she caught sight of
Leslie.

"What are you doing out of bed?" Marie demanded, holding a dripping wet umbrella away from
her body.

"I'm tired of lying in bed," Leslie mumbled, wincing inwardly at the petulant sound of her voice. "I'll
go out of my mind if I have to stay in that bed much
longer, Marie!"

"It's only been one week, Leslie." Though Marie sighed, her expression softened. "I know the inactivity grates on you more than most. You're always on the run," Marie commiserated. "But Leslie, you've got to stop fighting this. You're only prolonging your recovery."

"Yes, I know," Leslie murmured, acknowledging the wisdom of her friend's advice. "I'm sorry for causing you so much worry and trouble."

Marie scowled. "What trouble?"

Leslie met her scowl with a soft smile. "This is the third time this week that you've stopped by to check on me."

"No big deal." Marie grinned. "My mother-in-law is loving it. She's spoiling the very devil out of little Tony." She shrugged, and the movement shook cold drops of rain from the umbrella onto her legs. Marie grimaced and glanced down. "I'd better put this in the sink," she said, turning toward the small kitchen. "Can I get something for you?"

The very devil. The phrase bounced around in Leslie's mind, and a rueful smile shadowed her lips. She had met the very devil—and his name was Falcon. A shiver rippled through her body.

"Leslie?"

Marie's anxious voice pierced Leslie's distracted thoughts. "Yes?" Blinking, she focused on Marie, who was hovering in the kitchen doorway, brow knitted in alarm.

"Are you all right?" Marie demanded.

Leslie caught her lower lip between her teeth. Her behavior was deplorable, and she knew it. She was giving Marie the nervous fits. Crossing the room to her, Leslie grasped Marie's hand. "Yes, dear friend, I'm all right. I've been wallowing in self-pity, and I'm sorry."

"You're the least self-pitying person I know," Marie protested in a suspiciously husky voice. "Now," she went on with determined briskness, "how about a snack and a cup of coffee?"

"Okay," Leslie whispered, blinking rapidly to contain a fresh surge of tears. "If you'll let me have it in the kitchen and not that damn bed," she temporized, smiling and sniffing at the same time.

Marie shook her head and gave Leslie's hand a quick squeeze before releasing it and striding into the kitchen. "Boy, you don't give up, do you?" she chided, setting her umbrella in the sink. Turning around, she leveled a stern look at Leslie's wan face. "Will you at least sit down!" she exclaimed, shrugging out of her raincoat.

Positive that Marie would insist she return to bed the moment she'd finished eating, Leslie played for time by nibbling at her snack and raising different topics of conversation. When she ran out of chatter, she stalled by asking for more coffee.

By her expression, Marie made it clear to Leslie that she was on to her ploy. Still, she went along with it for a few minutes. "I'll run over next Thursday to bring you dinner," she said, getting up to refill Leslie's cup and then beginning to clear the table.

"Next Thursday?" Leslie repeated blankly.

Marie rolled her eyes. "Thanksgiving," she said distinctly. "You do remember Thanksgiving, don't you?"

Leslie frowned. "It is next Thursday, isn't it?" But before Marie could respond, Leslie shook her head vehemently. "No, Marie, it's not necessary. You'll have more than enough without worrying about me." She held up her hand when Marie would have argued. "I know you always have a houseful of relatives for the holiday. You'll be rushed off your feet. Besides, I have decided to contact an employment agency to hire someone to cook for me for the duration of this blasted illness."

"But—"

"Marie, I'll be fine," Leslie insisted. "You just enjoy the day with your family."

Marie was quiet as she finished clearing the dishes away. When they were stacked in the dishwasher and the kitchen restored to order, she stared at Leslie. "Speaking about family," she said. "Have you told your cousin Logan about your illness?"

"No!" Leslie exclaimed. "I know Logan McKittrick. If I called him, he and his wife Kit would very likely come tearing from Nevada to New York like a shot."

"Well, then, call him!" Marie said urgently. "He's all the family you have, and you need family now."

"No." Leslie's tone was adamant. "I imposed on Logan enough when I went running to him during the divorce. He and Kit aren't even married a full year, and they have the ranch to run." Her lips firmed. "I won't dump my troubles on him, Marie."

Knowing it was useless to argue with her friend, Marie subsided with a defeated sigh. "Boy, you certainly are bullheaded," she groused, then grinned. "But I can be just as determined." She pointed at the doorway. "Get back to bed," she ordered in the same stern-parent tone she used to correct her eighteen-month-old son.

Leslie exhaled dramatically, but gave in nonetheless. "Yes, mother," she muttered, rising and walking into the living room. She was nearing the short hallway that lead to her bedroom when the doorbell rang.

"I'll get it," Marie called, dashing out of the kitchen.

Tired but curious, Leslie paused in the hallway door, supporting her body by grasping the frame. Everything inside her seemed to freeze at the sound of the voice she heard when Marie opened the door.

"I'd like to see Ms. Fairfield, please. The name's Falcon."

Flint stared impassively at the young woman as her soft brown eyes widened in shock. Suppressing a dry smile and his mounting impatience, he waited silently for a response.

"Ah, hum, Leslie?"

The stuttering reply tested Flint's control. "Yes, Leslie," he said evenly. "She is here?" As he arched one dark eyebrow, he squashed an inner burst of panic. Leslie had to be here!

"Yes, she's here, but she's ill."

Flint let his pent-up breath escape on a soundless sigh of relief. "I know she's ill," he replied. "That's why I want to see her." Flint very deliberately narrowed his eyes. "May I come in?" His cool tone implied that there'd be hell to pay if she answered negatively. Satisfaction shimmered through him as the young woman backed up, pulling the door open as she did so.

"Well, I—yes, I guess so." As he crossed the threshold, she turned to glance over her shoulder. "Leslie, Mr. Falcon is here to see…" Her voiced faded as he walked by her.

Flint took two long strides into the room, then stopped cold, his narrowed gaze riveted on the woman who appeared to be clinging to the frame of a doorway leading off the living room.

Leslie! Flint stared at the pale imitation of the vivacious woman who had tormented every one of his hours, waking and sleeping, ever since he had watched her drive away from him five weeks ago. Leslie's vibrant beauty was now muted, like a bright day suddenly cast into shadow. The creamy skin Flint remembered had a fragile appearance, and her lips were colorless. The long, brilliant green eyes that had teased his memory were now dull and lifeless. The gorgeous flaming mane that he could still feel sliding silkily through his fingers had lost its luster.

What in God's name was the matter with her? he wondered, raw fear closing his throat. Flint was immobilized for an instant, gripped by a sense of stunned despair, a sensation he had not experienced since his trial, when he'd faced the jury and heard himself pronounced guilty as charged. At that long-ago time, Flint's despair had been swiftly overcome by raging anger. Now despair gave way to decisive action.

Striding to her, Flint caught Leslie's chin with carefully gentled fingers. "What the hell is wrong with you?" he demanded in a tone made deliberately harsh to conceal his clawing fear.

Leslie slowly lifted her chin away from his fingers. "I have mononucleosis," she answered in a choked voice. "And please don't ask me which college boy I've been kissing."

Affected more than he would have believed possible by her rejection of his touch, Flint's tone grew even more harsh. "I'm not a fool, Leslie. I'm aware of the growing number of diagnosed cases of mono in young adults and even middle-aged persons." His frown was fierce. "What I want to know is why aren't you in a hospital? You look awful."

"Thanks," Leslie muttered resentfully.

"Her doctor wanted to hospitalize her," the brown-eyed woman offered, "but she refused to go."

Flint glanced at the smaller woman, then back at Leslie with brows raised questioningly. Leslie responded to the prompt.

"Marie, as you already know, this is Flint Falcon." Staring into his eyes, she said, "Flint, my dearest friend, Marie Ferrini." Performing the introductions seemed to exhaust her. Alarm spread throughout Flint's body. It didn't show.

"You're caring for Leslie, Marie?" he asked, fighting hard to remain calm.

"No." Marie shook her head. "I stop in to see how she's doing."

Flint's lips tightened as he turned back to Leslie, but before he could comment, she jumped to her friend's defense.

"Marie has her own family to care for." She glared at him for a moment, reminding him vividly of the Leslie who'd shared his bed. Then the glitter in her green eyes faded, her lashes fluttered down and she sagged against the doorframe, scaring him into a fury.

"You're alone here?" he asked too softly.

The answer came from the woman behind Flint. "Yes, and she shouldn't be alone. She won't rest. I swear she needs a keeper."

"She just got one," Flint said with hard finality.

Leslie's eyes flew open. "I can take care of myself!"

"Oh, sure," Flint retorted grittily, "about as well as an hour-old infant." His lips twisted. "Lord, Leslie, you should see yourself. You look ready to fold up." He turned away as she opened her mouth to argue. "I'm taking her with me," he informed Marie in a flat tone. "I'd appreciate it if you'd help her pack some things."

"No!"

Leslie's protest went unheard by the man and woman staring at each other.

"You'll take care of her, make her rest?" Marie finally asked, apparently satisfied with whatever she saw in his expression.

"No." Leslie tried again and was again ignored.

"You have my word," Flint said firmly. Then a near-smile twitched his lips. "But, in addition to my word, if you'll give me your number I'll keep you informed as to her progress."

"No," Leslie moaned, turning her face to the wood frame.

"I'll help her get ready," Marie said, moving around him to go to Leslie.

Nine

You look awful. Ensconced in luxurious warmth in the back seat of the limo, Leslie listened to the swishing song of the tires on the rain-washed highway in a vain attempt to blot out the recurring sound of Flint's harsh voice echoing in her tired mind.

Why had he come to her now? she cried silently, burrowing into the silky fur lap robe Flint had so solicitously tucked around her after carrying her from her apartment to the car. Fur! The fingers clutching the robe flexed, digging into the sumptuous pelt. And not just any fur or fake fur, Leslie thought resentfully. Not just any common ordinary fur for Flint Falcon's comfort while traveling. His lap robe was fashioned of Russian lynx—silver, of course—which complemented the limo's black interior.

Why had he come to her now, when she looked *awful*? And why had he swept her away from New York after solemnly promising Marie he'd take care of her? Not once since their affair ended had Flint bothered to contact her. Why was he bothering now, when she looked and felt awful? The questions played leapfrog with the echo of Flint's harsh voice, exhausting her. The only answer that presented itself exhausted her even more.

Pity. The hateful word stabbed at Leslie's mind, and she flinched as if from a physical blow. She could not tolerate pity!

"Are you in pain?"

Leslie flinched again at the sound of Flint's voice. He was so near, seated so close to her in the roomy car that she could feel his thigh through the thick pile on the robe, so close and yet so far away. His nearness was the reason for her tightly shut eyes.

"Leslie, are you in pain?"

A demand for response underlined Flint's low tone, a demand her weakened resistance was not up to challenging. Refusing to look at him or answer vocally, Leslie moved her head back and forth against the seat, silently rejecting his presence and the compassion evident in his voice. She didn't want or need his damned pity or his compassion or his elegant black limousine with its ostentatious lap rug! Not now, when she could not meet him on equal terms, with equal strength.

Why had Marie abandoned her to him? The cry rang inside Leslie's head like the bewildered wail of a lost child. She had wept in the privacy of her bedroom, pleading with Marie to send Flint away. But, murmuring soothing words of assurance, Marie had bustled around, packing a suitcase, coaxing Leslie into slacks and a sweater, ignoring her pleas. She had stopped weeping when Marie had opened the bedroom door to call "She's ready" to Flint.

Hurt by her friend's betrayal, angered by Flint's arrogant imperiousness and drained of her last reserves of strength, Leslie retreated into resentful silence, refusing to respond in any way, even to Marie's fierce hug and tearfully whispered goodbye when the limo glided to a stop in front of Marie's apartment. Leslie had maintained her silent withdrawal throughout the hour they had been traveling since then, while inwardly screaming in protest.

"I know you're awake." Flint's quiet tone held infinite patience. "And I know you're angry with me for taking over the way I did." His sigh was barely perceptible, yet Leslie heard the long-suffering sound of it and her temper flared. "But, dammit, Leslie, what else could I do?"

Leslie didn't hear the odd, frightened note in Flint's voice. In her anger and her weakened condition, what she thought she heard was the lashing out of a man who felt himself trapped. "No one expected or asked you to do anything," she said in the coldest tone she could muster. "But right now you could have your driver turn around and take me home." Leslie had not given him the courtesy of opening her eyes to look at him while she spoke. Compounding the insult, she turned her face away from him. She clenched her teeth when she heard him sigh again.

"I can't do that," he said, his voice dropping lower. "We've got a long drive ahead. I suggest you try to sleep."

Sheer fury tore through Leslie, and with it a burst of energy. Her lashes swept up and the fire of rage glittered in her green eyes. Her voice was heavy with disdain.

"And I suggest that you go to hell, *Mr.* Falcon."

"I've been there." Flint's face was expressionless except for the wry smile that curved his thin lips. "It's a small place," he went on softly, "enclosed by three solid walls and a fourth made of bars."

Leslie immediately felt ashamed and would have apologized if he'd given her time, but he didn't.

"Go to sleep, Leslie." A flick of his hand indicated the space he'd put between them. "There's plenty of room for you to stretch out and get comfortable."

Swallowing against the lump of abject misery lodged in her inflamed throat, Leslie turned her head away again, this time in humiliation. Yet, resentment of his high-handedness burned within her and, determined not to fall asleep, she ignored his invitation to get comfortable. The minutes and miles spun by as Leslie fought the growing weight of her eyelids, but sleep claimed the final victory, easing her pain by possessing her consciousness.

The cessation of movement woke Leslie. Her body cramped, her mind confused, she stared at the dark tinted window. Where was she? Attempting to focus her bemused thoughts, she glanced around. A sense of relief and pure joy unfurled inside her as her gaze came to rest on Flint.

"Hello," he said, smiling gently. "We're here."

Here? Where? Leslie wondered. Then, in a rush, her senses cleared, her mind focused and reality slammed into her joy, shattering it into sharp shards of piercing disappointment.

"And where," she asked in a pain-dulled tone, "is here?"

"I'll explain later," Flint said briskly, pushing the door open. "Right now, I want to get you into the house and into bed." He stepped out of the car, issuing a terse order she couldn't hear to a person she couldn't see.

A moment later, the door next to her swung open and Flint leaned inside to carefully gather her into his arms, fur lap robe and all. Then, as carefully, he backed out of the car. Knowing it would be useless to do either, Leslie didn't struggle or protest.

It was dark and still raining, and to Leslie's wide-eyed surprise Flint's driver walked beside them, sheltering her beneath a large golf umbrella. Positioned between Flint and the driver, Leslie could see little except the outline of several buildings. But she could hear the sound of the surf and smell the distinct scent of the seashore. In that instant Leslie realized they were somewhere along the Jersey coast and, in all probability, not far from Atlantic City. Flint confirmed her conclusion when he dismissed the driver as he stepped through the open doorway into a house.

"Thanks, Rod," he said, glancing at the man over Leslie's head. "I won't need you anymore tonight. You may return to Falcon's Flight."

Leslie didn't hear the man's soft response; she was too busy studying the man and woman standing inside the small foyer. The man was small and slim, with shrewd eyes behind the dark-rimmed glasses perched on the bridge of his long, thin nose. The woman was tall and full-figured, with bright hazel eyes glowing in her smooth, attractive face.

"Is everything prepared?" Flint asked the man.

"Exactly as you ordered, Flint," the man replied at once. "Mrs. Knox has everything under control," he said, turning toward the woman.

"Mrs. Knox." Flint nodded once. "Thank you for coming on such short notice."

"You're welcome, Mr. Falcon." Mrs. Knox smiled and glanced at Leslie. "If you'll bring Ms. Fairfield in here—" she indicated the living room to the right of the foyer "—I'll make her comfortable, then serve dinner."

Though Leslie felt extremely comfortable cradled in Flint's strong arms, his scent and closeness were driving her senses into spasm. Offering Mrs. Knox a hesitant smile, she murmured, "I am hungry."

Her small statement activated the trio. Spinning on her heel, Mrs. Knox led the way into the spacious living room. Flint followed the woman. The small man trailed Flint. Mrs. Knox came to a stop near the end of a long couch made up into a bed. Flint came to a stop beside the couch and eased Leslie to her feet. The small man stood by, his expression alert.

"Do you feel at all rested from your nap in the car?" Flint asked in a low voice as he removed first the lap robe and then her coat.

Leslie frowned at him, but answered truthfully. "Yes, some." Her frown deepened as she glanced around. "Where are we?"

"I'll explain everything over dinner," Flint murmured, glancing at the older woman. "As you heard, Leslie, this is Mrs. Knox, my housekeeper." He turned away as Leslie smiled tentatively at the woman. "If you'll get Ms. Fairfield settled, Mrs. Knox, I'll change and be back in a few minutes." At the woman's nod, he shifted his gaze to the small man. "You come with me, Keith."

Mrs. Knox began fussing over Leslie the moment the men stepped out of the room. Within minutes the woman had whisked off Leslie's clothing and shoes and was gently bullying her into a nightgown and the emerald-green robe. She smiled at Leslie as she gathered up the discarded clothes.

"Now you just snuggle under the covers there on the couch, Ms. Fairfield," she said pleasantly. "I'll bring you your dinner right after I put these things away."

Bursting with questions but with nobody left to address them to, Leslie gave a fatalistic shrug and did as she was bidden. She was stretching her long legs the length of the couch when Flint strode back into the room, his small shadow a pace behind him.

"Better?" he asked, gazing down at her as he halted beside the couch. Flint had exchanged his dark three-piece suit for casual slacks and a sweater that showed off his trim body and did weird things to her pulse rate.

"Yes," she breathed on a sigh. Then she added softly, "Thank you."

"You're welcome," he returned as softly, the tension visibly easing from his austere expression. "And you'll continue to get better from now on," he assured her. "I'll see to it." He angled his head to look at the small man. "Or we will. Right, Keith?"

"Right, Flint." Keith's solemn expression relaxed in a charming smile. "Beginning with the specialist tomorrow morning."

"Specialist?" Leslie repeated. "What specialist?"

"The one who's going to examine you tomorrow," Flint said reasonably. "And don't argue," he warned. Then, remembering his oversight, he said, "By the way, Leslie, this is my secretary, Keith Bowers. He keeps my business wheels oiled." He motioned the man forward. "Keith, say hello to Ms. Fairfield."

"Leslie," she instructed before he could respond. "Hello, Keith, and do you keep Flint's wheels well oiled?"

"Well, let's say I run around behind him with the oilcan. Hello, Leslie." Leaning over, he extended his hand. Keith's grip was firm; his smile was friendly. "I've admired your work for some time; it's a pleasure to finally meet you."

"Why, thank you, Keith, I—"

"Dinner," Flint interrupted to announce. "Keith, get out of here, and my apologies to your lady friend for making you late. I'll be in touch in the morning." As Flint was speaking, he was also arranging a table and chair next to the couch. Keith was leaving through one door while the housekeeper entered through another.

Mrs. Knox served the meal, then disappeared into the kitchen. Leslie was full of questions for Flint, but the delicious aroma of roast beef and Yorkshire pudding sent every one of them out of her mind. Sitting on the edge of the couch, she dug into the food but very quickly had to slow down, amazed at how tiring the simple act of eating had become. Fortunately, she successfully concealed her weakness from Flint.

Flint was quiet until after Mrs. Knox had removed the dishes, served coffee and disappeared again. Then, when he did begin speaking, it was to chastise Leslie for not following her doctor's instructions to the letter.

"I thought you had more sense," he concluded, obviously exasperated.

Leslie's eyes welled with tears, which she brushed away impatiently. "I did! I do! Oh, I don't know!" she cried in frustration.

"Well, that certainly clears everything up," Flint drawled, lips twitching in amusement.

"Are you laughing at me?" Leslie demanded.

"Me?" Flint's eyebrows rose. "Wouldn't dream of it." The twitch tugged harder at his lips.

Though Leslie fought it, her lips curved into a sheepish smile. "I've behaved irresponsibly, haven't I?"

"Quite," Flint agreed, but he softened the cold word with a smile. "That's why I decided to take over. You do understand that you were only prolonging your recovery," he continued in a gentle tone, "don't you?"

Leslie lowered her gaze from his watchful eyes. "Yes," she admitted in a whisper. "But I did so want to do that play," she added on a sad sigh.

"There'll be other plays, Leslie," Flint murmured. "But first you must get well." His pause was brief. "Will you let me help you do that?"

Now he asks me! Leslie thought, fully aware that she'd have given him a firm no if he had bothered to ask before. Glancing up, she met his intent gaze. "Yes, Flint," she responded meekly, proving her willingness by setting her cup aside and stretching out again on the couch.

"Good." Flint refilled his coffee cup, then lounged back in his chair. He moved his hand to indicate their surroundings. "We are in Longport, some fifteen or so minutes south of Atlantic City. This house is mine; I inherited it from my paternal grandfather." His lips firmed. "I intend to keep you here until you've completely recovered from this infection—regardless of how long it takes."

"Why?" Leslie asked, uncertain if she really wanted to hear the answer. It was not what she'd expected.

"Why?" Flint grinned, stealing her breath. "Because, as Marie so accurately said, you need a keeper."

Depression settled on Leslie. She didn't want a keeper. She wanted to be a keeper, a keeper woman, the one woman a Falcon would want to keep by his side for the rest of his life. But if Leslie had learned nothing else over the previous weeks, she had come to the realization that this particular Falcon valued his freedom above all else. Accepting the fact was not easy for Leslie—she loved him. But it was essential that she accept his reasons for helping her. When she was once again well, Flint would return her to New York, then fly away from her.

"Leslie?" As he had weeks before, Flint called to her softly so as not to wake her if she'd fallen asleep.

"Yes?" Leslie raised her gaze to his. Flint misread the pain mirrored in her eyes.

"I do understand how important your independence is to you, and I admire you for it," he said. "But you do see that you can't be alone, don't you?"

"Yes." Leslie lowered her eyes again.

"Would you prefer to go to a hospital?" There was a strange tautness to his voice that Leslie couldn't identify. The sound of it drew her gaze back to his.

"No," she said quickly.

"Okay." The strange tautness was gone, replaced by an even stranger note of satisfaction. "We'll take good care of you, Mrs. Knox and I," he promised.

It didn't take very long for Leslie to realize how very well Flint kept his promises.

"There, is that better?" Flint asked softly, stepping back from the couch.

"Yes." Leslie lowered her eyes. "Thank you."

Ten days of complete rest free from stress had wrought a dramatic change in Leslie. She wasn't quite as pale and drawn, and the bouts of tears and depression had abated somewhat. She had been cosseted and comforted by both Flint and Mrs. Knox and was showing marked results because of their care.

Subsiding into the pillows Flint placed behind her head, Leslie examined her surroundings with interest. She had been too ill and too distracted that first night to notice much about the house other than the guest bedroom Flint had carried her to soon after they'd finished dinner. The following morning Flint had bundled her into the limo for the short run into Atlantic City to see the specialist. After a thorough examination and blood tests, the doctor had confirmed the diagnosis made by Leslie's own physician. He prescribed the same treatment as well, bed rest, an antibiotic to ward off the possibility of bacterial throat infection and aspirin to reduce fever and discomfort. The specialist had also offered Leslie an incentive.

"If you'll follow my instructions to the letter, Ms. Fairfield," he'd said sternly, "you could be well by Christmas."

With his words ringing in her head, Leslie had docilely allowed Mrs. Knox to help her into bed on her return to the house. She had spent every day since then in bed.

"Well?" Seated in a chair he'd drawn close to the couch, Flint smiled wryly as he observed her intent gaze on the portrait above the fireplace.

"Is that your father?" Leslie asked, frowning as she looked at him, then back at the portrait. The resemblance was uncanny, and had it not been for the difference in hair color, Leslie would have believed the painting was of Flint.

"My grandfather," Flint said, his expression softening as he gazed at the portrait. "He practically raised me."

While Flint stared at the picture, Leslie stared at him. The change in his usually severe expression was startling. Flint's face was free of strain and his eyes were dark. Gone was the aura of frightening intimidation. His face revealed painful acceptance. Observing him, Leslie felt a surge of love and compassion for the lonely man gazing out of the eyes of the indomitable Flint Falcon.

"You loved him very much," Leslie murmured, blinking against a rush of tears that had nothing to do with her illness.

"Yes, I loved him very much." Flint's lips tilted into a bittersweet smile. "He died three years ago; I think a part of me died with him." A soft sigh escaped his lips and he continued to speak, softly, as if he'd forgotten she was there. "Everything I am, everything I have accomplished is a result of his loving care and wise counsel." He exhaled harshly. "And I don't even bear his name."

"But why not?" Leslie asked. But before he could respond, she said, "Oh! He was your mother's father?"

"No." Flint reluctantly drew his gaze from the portrait to look at her, the more familiar wry smile curving his lips. "It's a long story."

"I'm not going anywhere," Leslie said in a dry tone.

Flint's lips twitched as he ran his gaze the length of her body reclining on the couch. "No, I don't suppose you are," he agreed, grinning at her.

"So indulge me." Leslie arched her brows imperiously. "Tell me a story."

His grin widened and his eyes brightened with a teasing gleam. "Well, once upon a time . . ." he began in the time-honored way.

"Falcon," Leslie said in a warning tone. Pushing herself into a sitting position, she swung her legs to the floor.

Flint's amusement vanished. "Leslie, don't you dare get up!" Springing out of his chair, Flint grasped her legs and swung them onto the couch. "You promised to behave if I brought you downstairs." His eyes were hard. "Do you want to undo all the progress you've made?"

"No." Leslie shook her head. "I'm sorry, Flint." Leslie's eyes filled with the symptomatic tears she had begun to hope were a thing of the past.

"Leslie, don't cry." Dropping to his knees, Flint drew her into his arms. "I didn't mean to upset you," he murmured, stroking her hair. "I want you to get well."

"Oh, Flint!" Hiding her face against his shoulder, Leslie cried softly. "I hate this! I hate feeling weepy and weak and depressed. And I hate taking you away from your work, being a burden on you."

"That's enough!" Tilting her face up, Flint stared into her eyes. "You are not taking me from my work. I can run my business very well with the telephone and the periodic trips I make into Atlantic City." Lowering his head, he caught an escaping tear with his lips. "And you are not a burden," he murmured against her cheek. Drawing back, he smiled rakishly at her. "The only burden has been being with you, without being *with* you."

Leslie's eyes filled again. "I look dreadful," she moaned. "You couldn't possibly want me in that way!"

"I want you in every way." Flint took her mouth with hungry demand, shocking and alarming her.

"Flint!" Leslie cried, pulling away from him. "I'm probably still contagious!"

Flint laughed. "Look at it this way," he said. "If I get mono, we can recuperate together. At least then we could share the same bed."

"You're terrible," Leslie laughed.

"And you love it," he retorted.

"Yes, I do," she admitted, her smile fading. "Because I love you." The admission had slipped past her guard. Appalled at herself, Leslie stared at him, waiting for his expression to close, locking her out. To her disbelief and wonder, Flint smiled.

"Are you trying to drive me crazy by telling me that now, knowing I can't drag you off to my bed?"

"No." Leslie lowered her eyes. "I want you to drag me off to your bed."

"You witchy redhead!" Releasing her, Flint sank back into his chair, laughter exploding from his throat. "I believe you really are trying to drive me crazy." He stopped laughing abruptly. "The damned thing is, I think you're succeeding."

"Am I?" Try as she might, Leslie couldn't keep the note of hope from her tone.

"Don't crowd me, darling, let me work this out for myself. Okay?"

Leslie nodded. She had no choice in the matter; the wariness was back in his eyes and in his tone. "Okay, Flint." Sighing, she settled down against the pillows. "I promise I'll be good."

"You already are good; that's the problem," Flint muttered. Then his voice turned brisk. "And to help you rest, I'll tell you a bedtime story." He smiled wryly. "It's so boring it'll probably put you to sleep."

"Try me," Leslie challenged.

"You were right on target," he said, stretching his long legs out in front of him, "when you called me a bastard." He went on to explain when she frowned in confusion, "I am legally a bastard. That's why I never bore my grandfather's name."

"Oh, Flint, I'm so sorry!" Leslie said softly.

"I might have been, too, if it hadn't been for him."
Flint inclined his head toward the portrait. When she
frowned again, he smiled. "I'd better begin at the beginning. My father was a geologist and worked for a
company with interests all over the world. He met and
fell in love with my mother while on assignment in
New Mexico." He paused, then smiled. "My mother
is a Navajo and proud of it."

"Understandably," Leslie murmured.

"Don't interrupt," Flint chided. "At any rate, they
fell in love and became lovers. He asked her to marry
him. She said yes. But before they had time to make
plans my father was given another top-priority assignment. Within a few days he was on his way to
South America. The corporate plane he was in flew
into the side of a mountain during a severe thunder-
storm. He never even knew that my mother had con-
ceived his child."

"Your mother never saw him again?"

"No," Flint sighed. "She had received a letter he
had written to her the night before he boarded that
plane in Rio. And that might have been the last she
ever heard of him, except that he had written to his
parents as well. And that's where my grandfather entered the picture."

Flint turned a gaze at the painting. He was quiet a
long time, and when he began talking again it was as
if he was speaking to the man he so obviously loved.
"In his letter, my father had told his parents about the
wonderful young woman he had fallen in love with
and was planning to marry as soon as possible. And
so, after receiving notification of his death, my
grandfather flew to New Mexico. He called my mother

his daughter. They wept in each other's arms. My mother loved and honored him until the day she died."

"Your mother's dead, too?"

The sympathy in Leslie's voice drew his gaze from the portrait. "Yes. She lived long enough to see me graduate from college. She died loving my father." His gaze drifted back to the painting. "And his father."

"As you did and still do," Leslie said softly.

"Yes." Flint looked at her and smiled. "I spent every winter here in New Jersey with my grandparents. The summers I spent with my mother in New Mexico." His smile deepened. "My mother's father named me Flint because of the odd color of my eyes." He laughed softly. "He gave me the name Falcon, too. He said there was a fierce wildness about me from the minute I opened my eyes."

"Can the Falcon be held?" Leslie asked tightly.

Flint's lips slanted into the familiar wry smile. "The Falcon is wild, you know. Are you sure you want to hold him?"

"Very sure," she responded immediately. "I'm just not sure how to do it."

"As with all birds that love to soar," he murmured, "you hold on to them with open hands."

Ten

───

"Feeling feisty, are you?"

Leslie glanced up from the script she'd been reading, a brilliant smile illuminating her face. "Flint!" A flush of pleasure gave color to her still slightly pale cheeks. "I didn't hear you come up the stairs."

"Obviously," Flint remarked dryly, strolling to the foot of the bed. "Going somewhere?" he asked, pointedly scrutinizing her appearance. Her hair gleamed with highlights, her newly manicured fingernails were tinged with pink polish, her lips shimmered with recently applied gloss. In Flint's unvoiced opinion, the lipstick was a sure sign of Leslie's rapidly improving health.

"Well, I had considered joining Donald Trump for lunch," Leslie replied in a dry tone, casting a significant glance over her nightgowned form ensconced in the bed. "But then this script arrived from my agent—'' she held the article aloft ''—and I simply forgot about lunch.'' Leslie sighed. ''I'm sure he's crushed.''

A teasing smile quirked Flint's lips. ''Serves him right for inviting my lady to lunch in the first place,'' he observed, mildly amazed at his inner reaction to the bantering remark. Flint was unfamiliar with the uncomfortable sensations aroused by jealousy, yet he identified the emotion immediately. Jealous! Him? Ridiculous. Refusing to acknowledge the mere thought of himself as a jealous lover, Flint walked to the side of the bed to place a large manila envelope by her side.

''What's this?'' Leslie arched her brows and set the script aside.

''The mail that's been accumulating at your apartment. Marie sent it to my office.'' Flint shrugged. ''I was going to send somebody down with it, but since I was planning to come down anyway, I decided to hold it and bring it with me.'' Flint consoled himself with the fact that at least part of his urbanely delivered statement was true. The literal truth was that he'd been raking his mind for an excuse to visit her. Not that he needed an excuse, he had repeatedly reminded himself; it was, after all, his house. But, for the past seventeen days, ever since Leslie had told him she was in love with him, Flint had kept his distance. It wasn't that he was hiding out in his aerie in Atlantic City, he assured himself confidently, it was merely that he needed some time to adjust to the change in status between them. Complicating his emotional dilemma was the very real and uncomfortable hunger he had for her, a hunger that increased painfully with each successive visit he made to the house. Flint had decided that it would be more dignified to keep his distance than to abase himself by joining her in her sickbed.

Now, watching in silence as she riffled through her correspondence, Flint experienced a startling but pleasant glow of inner warmth. Leslie was almost well. He could discern shadings of her former vibrance and animation. The sparkle of life was back in her fabulous green eyes. And only now, some four weeks since he'd rushed to her after reading that notice in the gossip column, could Flint acknowledge the depth of alarm he'd felt at the sight of her pale appearance.

Strangely, though he could feel the silken threads beginning to close around him, caging him in, Flint felt no threatening sense of entrapment. Studying Leslie's rapt expression as she read what appeared to be some sort of invitation, Flint felt relief because of her improving physical condition and an odd but rather pleasant sense of contentment.

"J.B.'s getting married!"

Leslie's exclamation scattered Flint's introspective thoughts. "That's nice. Who's J.B.?" he asked, smiling in response to the delight shining from her eyes.

"A very caring, thoughtful friend," she murmured, her eyes growing misty with memory. "I met him in Las Vegas last year. I'm glad he has found someone. I only hope she's good enough for him."

Flint could feel his hackles rising as envy of this *caring, thoughtful* friend of Leslie's started to fill him. Telling himself to cool off, Flint managed to keep his smile in place. "I assume that's an invitation to the wedding?" He inclined his head to indicate the oversized card in her hand.

"Yes." Leslie held it out to him. "It's a Christmas wedding. It should be beautiful," she said enthusiastically.

"Umm," he murmured, lowering his gaze to read the elaborate print. The invitation requested the honor of Leslie's presence at the Christmas Eve candlelight ceremony of marriage to be held in a church in Philadelphia. "It probably will be beautiful," Flint agreed, handing the invitation back to her.

"I want to go." Flint stiffened, but before he could respond she grasped his hand and went on, "Flint, please, can we go?"

Her use of the plural *we* was his undoing. Ridiculously pleased by having her link them as a unit, he felt the tension ease out of him and he smiled. "We'll ask the doctor when you go in for your appointment next week. If he says it will be safe for you to go, I'll take you to Philadelphia."

"Oh, Flint, thank you!" Leslie cried, tossing off the covers and flinging herself into his arms.

As a reward, Flint reflected, crushing her warm body to his chest, Leslie's form of showing gratitude beat breaking the bank at Monte Carlo.

What a Christmas present! Shivering with excitement, Leslie could barely sit still in the limo's back seat. Moments before, she had fairly danced to the car from her doctor's office. That wonderful man had pronounced her cured! She didn't want to sit in regal state inside the black stretch limo; Leslie wanted to run and play!

"I want to go to the casino," she said imperiously, deliberately banishing the entreating tone that had colored her voice while she'd been weak and ill. She had determined she would not deal with Flint on any other than equal terms. Tilting her head, Leslie gave him an arch look. For all her assumed haughtiness, Flint Falcon took her breath away.

"Really?" he drawled, raising one dark eyebrow. "Any casino in particular?"

Though she did try, Leslie couldn't maintain her air of cool indifference. She simply felt too, too—*healthy*! "Oh, Flint, I feel so good!" She laughed. "I want to visit every casino, but yours in particular."

Raising his hand, Flint slid his fingers into the silky strands of her hair, tugging gently to urge her closer to him. "I understand how you feel," he said, leaning over to touch his lips to her glowing cheek. "But remember, the doctor told you not to overextend yourself. Moderation, Leslie," he cautioned, drawing her into his arms. "You should conserve your energy. We've got that trip up to Philly at the end of the week."

"I know." Sighing, Leslie snuggled into his hard strength. Lifting her head, she gazed into his unusual eyes and got lost in the blue-gray depths. "Okay," she murmured dreamily. "I'll settle for an hour and a half at one casino—yours. Deal?" His soft laughter added an element of anticipation to her excitement.

"It's a deal," he agreed, brushing his lips over hers. "And when you've finished playing, we'll have a long, relaxing dinner—" he paused to give her a slow smile "—in my apartment."

It was not yet two in the afternoon and the casino was packed. Meandering aimlessly through the large room, Leslie felt mildly surprised by her lack of interest in the play around her. Where was the old thrill of anticipation she had expected to feel? she wondered. She had always been able to divorce herself from stress by stepping into any casino. And though she was feeling strong and well again, she was tense. Leslie fully realized that when the doctor released her from his care, he had in effect released her from Flint's care as well.

It was time for Leslie to go home, back to her own apartment and back to work. She had infringed on Flint long enough. Glancing around the casino, Flint's casino, a smile curved Leslie's lips. She didn't need this avenue of escape any longer, she thought, turning toward an exit. She had done a lot of growing during the past year, most of it within the weeks she'd spent confined to bed. She loved Flint with every beat of her heart, but if it didn't work out for them she knew she would not fall apart. It would hurt, but she would survive—without an escape hatch.

Suddenly eager to get on with her life, Leslie strode from the casino to the lobby, where Flint had said he'd be waiting for her. She needed to call Marie and her agent, and she needed to be with Flint, because she really didn't know how much time she had left to be with him. She decided that it would be extremely stupid of her to waste precious moments by playing games.

Flint was waiting for her exactly where he'd said he would be. He greeted her with a smile that caused a major flurry in her midsection. "Lose all your money already?"

"No." Leslie returned his smile and slid her arm through his. "I'd like to make a few phone calls in private, and I want that dinner you promised me." She tugged on his arm to get him moving in the direction of the elevator. "Besides, there are too many people in there."

"Bite your tongue, woman," he said. "As far as I'm concerned, there can never be *too* many people in my casino."

Leslie gazed around at the very elegant interior and the mass of people jostling for position to register at the desk. "It's already a smashing success for you, isn't it?" she asked, returning her gaze to his face.

"Yes." Flint didn't smile, and his tone was without inflection, yet Leslie could sense his satisfaction. She did smile, brightly, sincerely.

"I'm glad." And she was, even though she knew that Falcon's Flight, and what it represented to Flint, was more of a rival than the most enchanting of other women.

Stepping into Flint's apartment gave Leslie a warmer sense of homecoming than she'd ever experienced on returning to her own place. Fighting a growing melancholy, she kept her smile bright and her step light. Tossing her purse onto a chair, she walked directly to the phone, arching her brows at Flint as she reached for the receiver. "May I?"

Heading for the stairs, Flint paused to slant a wry smile at her. "Of course," he said, taking the stairs two at a time. "I'll order our dinner from my office phone."

Marie was delighted to hear of Leslie's complete recovery. Her agent was delighted to hear that Leslie was ready to go back to work and that she loved the script he'd sent to her. Leslie was delighted that everyone was delighted. She was inwardly battling encroaching depression.

Dinner was long and relaxing and utterly delicious. The wine was crisp and refreshing. Flint's eyes were dark with unspoken promises that set off tiny fires in Leslie's body that thoroughly consumed her feeling of mellow well-being.

Gazing into his face, Leslie sighed and held out her arms to him. At that moment she loved him so much, wanted to be part of him so badly, that her bones ached.

"If you don't come over here and kiss me at once," she whispered, "I'm afraid I might have a relapse."

"I wouldn't want to be the cause of that." Flint was out of his chair and bending over her before he'd finished speaking. "You're like a moody child when you're ill," he teased, his hands gentle as he drew her out of her chair and into his arms. "And, though the child is adorable," he murmured as he lowered his head to hers, "I much prefer the woman."

Flint's mouth was tender yet hungry on hers. His hands moved lightly but restlessly over her quivering body. His heart pounded against hers. Releasing her mouth, he swept her up into his arms and strode toward the stairs.

"I vowed I wouldn't rush you," he said in a strained voice as he walked into his bedroom and nudged the door shut with his heel. "And the last thing I want is to upset you," he muttered, settling her in the center of the bed and covering her body with his. "But, God, Leslie, it's been two months, and I've discovered I don't handle celibacy well," he groaned against her lips.

Two months! Leslie's spirits soared with hope. Flint had not been with a woman since the day their affair ended! And she was certain he had not remained celibate because of a lack of opportunity; Leslie had witnessed his effect on women. Bubbling with happiness, melting with love for him, she clasped his head with her hands and drew his mouth to hers.

"You want to know a secret?" she murmured, brushing her lips over his. "I've very recently discovered that I don't handle celibacy well, either."

Flint's soft, sexy laughter sent tingles of excitement scurrying through her body, his stroking touch engulfed her in flames, his kiss sent her senses whirling out of control. Everything that was Leslie was Flint's, her body, her mind, her soul.

Freely, joyously, Leslie helped Flint cast off the barrier of their clothing. Then, sighing her pleasure in surrender, she helped him join their bodies in the ancient, most sacred celebration of life.

A twelve-foot blue spruce blazing with hundreds of tiny white lights stood majestically next to the choir section. A profusion of poinsettia plants flanked the candlelit altar. The organ vibrated with chords of a traditional song about love and devotion. The setting was perfect for the most solemn of vows to be exchanged between a man and a woman. Leslie's eyes were misty with tears.

The magnificent old Philadelphia church was rapidly filling with elegantly attired guests, none of whom came close to equaling the man seated beside Leslie. Loving Flint more deeply with each successive day, Leslie was profoundly moved by her surroundings and the occasion requiring her presence in the church.

A low murmur rippling through the guests drew her attention. Blinking to clear her vision, Leslie glanced around. A soft smile of recognition curved her lips and grew to a smile of delight as her gaze came to rest on a tall, lovely young woman with hair the shade of spun silver. The woman was glowing with pregnancy. The tall, rugged-looking man at her side was beaming with pride.

"Well, I'll be—!" Flint exclaimed in a hushed tone.

"Do you know them?" Leslie asked in a shocked whisper.

"Not very well," Flint responded, watching their progress. "I bought my Lake Tahoe casino from the woman. I was never formally introduced to the man." Flint frowned. "Do you know them?"

"Yes," Leslie whispered. "The proud papa-to-be is my cousin, Logan McKittrick. The woman is his wife and my friend, Kit."

"I knew their names," Flint drawled. "They appear to be very happy," he went on, slowly, almost reluctantly. "When did they get married?"

"A year ago," she murmured, raising her hand slightly to acknowledge the couple's surprised but pleased reaction as they noticed her. Their startled expressions made it clear that they recognized Flint as well. The usher seated the couple in the pew directly in front of her, and Leslie was leaning forward to murmur a greeting when a stronger rustle moved through the guests. Curious, Leslie glanced around, a warm smile again touching her lips.

The man and woman would have created a stir in any crowd. The man was extremely tall and extraordinarily handsome, with bronzed skin and a shock of gold hair on his head and a thin line of a gold beard on his firm jaw. The woman was much smaller, her delicate beauty framed by a waist-long mane of shimmering jet-black hair. Yet what drew female sighs were the two identical black-haired infants solemnly gazing at the assemblage out of wide dark-brown eyes.

"You know them also?" Flint murmured, noting her nod of greeting.

"The man," Leslie said. "He is Kit's half brother, Zackery Sharp. I've never met his wife. Her name is Aubrey."

"Lovely."

Leslie turned to face him, eyebrows arched. "The woman or her name?"

"Both." Flint's lips twitched. "They also appear very happily married."

"Amazing, isn't it?" she drawled. Before Flint could retaliate, Kit was turning in her seat to whisper to Leslie.

"The man being seated on the other side is the bride's brother. His wife is the matron of honor," she said in a whisper, offering Flint a charming smile. Leslie saw Flint smile in return as she swiveled to look at the new arrivals.

The tall, dark-haired man came darned close to matching Flint in the appearance of imperious intimidation. He was handsome in an aristocratic, patrician way.

"Another happily married duo?" Flint wondered aloud.

"He certainly looks smug and content," Leslie whispered sweetly.

"Umm," he murmured, glancing away. "And who's this?" he asked a moment later. "A young mother without a husband in tow?"

Leslie shifted her interested gaze to the beautiful auburn-haired woman being ushered down the aisle, a baby girl of about six months held securely in her arms. An older, fiercely erect woman walked by her side.

Obviously having overheard Flint's comment, Kit turned in the pew to offer enlightenment and a gentle reprimand. "Her name is Barbara, Mr. Falcon. The other woman is her Aunt Ellie. The baby's name is Rita. The husband is not in tow because he's the best man. He's also my other half brother, the other half of a matched set—Zackery's twin, Thackery, the groom's best friend." Losing the battle against a smile at the sound of her husband's soft laughter, Kit settled herself decorously on the pew.

"Zackery and Thackery?" Flint repeated. "Oh, good grief!"

From in front of Flint came a choking noise; then Logan's shoulders shook with suppressed laughter. Within seconds, Flint's shoulders were duplicating the action. Leslie and Kit scolded simultaneously, if softly.

"Flint!"

"Logan!"

Fortunately, at that moment the bride's mother was seated and the groom and best man came out of a side door and walked to the end of the aisle, upon which two men were quickly unrolling a white runner.

"Joshua Barnet, I take it?" Flint said, quoting the name that had been imprinted on the wedding invitation.

"Yes, J.B." Leslie smiled, studying the sharply angled face of the man who had been the friend she'd needed while recovering from divorce. Unsurprisingly, a similar soft smile curved Kit's lips.

Although some inches shorter in height than his best man, J.B.'s dark good looks and whipcord-lean body was in no way overshadowed by the handsome blond giant standing by his side.

"The other half of the matched set sports a mustache instead of a narrow beard," Flint observed. "And your friend J.B. has the look of a very tough customer when riled," he judged astutely.

Leslie opened her mouth to defend her friend, but at that instant the opening bars preceding the wedding march swelled from the organ. As one, the guests rose and turned to face the back of the church. Her steps measured, her bearing regal, the tall, beautiful matron of honor appeared to glide down the white path, her holly-green gown a perfect foil for her cool blond loveliness. When she had reached the midway point of the aisle, soft *ohs* and *ahs* blended with the music. All eyes were riveted on the couple starting down the aisle.

One delicate hand resting on the arm of her distinguished-looking father, the bride, Nicole Vanzant, walked down the aisle like a queen, her bright gaze never veering from the tanned face of her groom. Her gown was an artist's creation of white silk and hand-made lace. Her pearl-encrusted headpiece crowned her dark hair. The filmy veil covering her face could not conceal the perfection of her features.

Slowly turning as she followed the bride's progress, Leslie felt a knot of emotion fill her throat as she caught sight of J.B.'s face. His expression was etched into lines of near-adoration for the woman walking to him. Unabashed love blazed from his dark eyes.

Tears rolled unchecked down Leslie's face as she listened to the couple exchange their vows. She felt as if the depth of meaning of the words was being inscribed on her soul.

"With this ring I thee wed."

Then the voices faded, and Leslie's heart seemed to stop beating as Flint's palm slid over hers and he gently entwined their fingers, symbolically joining them just as the pastor's voice broke through her bemusement.

"What God has joined together, let no man put asunder."

It was obvious upon arrival that the wedding reception had been carefully planned to be a rather formal affair. Fortunately, the groom's assortment of family and friends swiftly turned it into a congenial, enjoyable celebration.

With Flint by her side, Leslie circulated among the guests, introducing him to her family and her friends, smiling as she and Flint were in turn introduced to those she was unacquainted with. Strangely, Flint was utterly charming to everyone outside Leslie's own small circle of friends, yet exchanged cool, wary glances with the men within that circle. Caught between bafflement and amusement, Leslie watched the male measuring process with fascination.

Logan McKittrick was terse, but not exactly hostile; Flint responded in kind.

The blond twin giants Thack and Zack Sharp scrutinized him from shrewd, narrowed eyes; Flint returned their scrutiny with eyes as unaffected and remote as the North Sea. Even Nicole's brother, Peter Vanzant, ran a haughtily appraising glance the length of Flint's impeccably attired person; Flint's namesake eyes glittered with a like assessment. But the most thorough and comprehensive examination of Flint was made by the groom, the tough-looking police captain, J.B. Barnet. Flint endured the visual dissection for a full sixty seconds. Then, slowly moving his steady gaze around the circle of unfriendly male faces, he effortlessly broke the ice with J.B. and the rest of the men.

"Would you care to step outside as a group or one by one?" Flint drawled sardonically.

Logan broke first. A blatant male grin curved his lips. "If any of you decide to accomodate him," he said, echoing Flint's drawl, "I suggest you wear your armor." He sliced an amused glance at Flint. "I've seen the way this man handles a knife."

For Leslie, the party was a smashing success. By the time it was over, Flint had been completely accepted by her family and friends, old and new. In fact, a stranger could have been forgiven for mistaking Flint, Logan, J.B., Thack, Zack and even Peter for drinking buddies of long standing. Though happy, Leslie was also thankful for Flint's insistence on being driven to Philadelphia in the limo.

At two o'clock Christmas morning, the limo delivered them to the curb in front of Leslie's Manhattan apartment. Flint sent their driver to a hotel, then followed her to her apartment, her suitcase in one hand, her fingers encased in the other.

For two days, Leslie and Flint did nothing but eat and sleep and make love. And if they ate and slept very little, well...their lovemaking was all the nourishment and rest they seemed to need. Without the words being spoken aloud, Leslie knew that Flint would not stay with her any length of time. She didn't have to hear the words; he said it with the intensity of his lovemaking. She had steeled herself to accept the words when they finally were spoken late on their second night together.

"I must leave in the morning. I have appointments I can't put off any longer." Flint's voice was low and strained, but steady as a rock. "The car will be here for me at seven." He hesitated, then added softly, "I would like you to sleep in."

"All right," she agreed, burying her face in the curve of his shoulder. Leslie knew why he'd made the request; Flint was afraid that at the last minute she would beg him to stay with her. And Leslie wanted to—Lord, how she wanted to—but she hadn't forgotten her question to him of how to hold on to a falcon, nor had she forgotten his answer.

Leslie didn't have to break her promise to Flint to sleep in, simply because they never went to sleep in the first place. But she did remain in bed, watching his every move as he prepared to leave. At seven exactly he glanced out the window, then turned and walked to the bed. His kiss was so very tender it brought tears to her eyes. It was also very brief.

"This time I will call you," he whispered against her trembling lips. "I promise I will."

"I know you will." Smiling at him, Leslie deliberately opened her hands, releasing the hold she had on either side of his face. And then he was gone.

Flint stood unmoving before the window wall in his office. All was silent; the sound of revelry from far below could not penetrate the heights to his private aerie. Flint knew that noise and merrymaking filled the casino and every lounge, ballroom, private suite and room throughout the hotel. He knew and did not care. Through the window before him, clouds scur-

ried across a black winter sky and the moon cut a
swath of silver into the restless ocean. And it was his,
but there was something missing.

Flint Falcon had defined the difference between
being alone and being lonely. Narrowing his eyes, Flint
projected images onto that black panorama. He could
see a church ablaze with Christmas splendor, and a
woman in glistening white walking toward a man with
love shining from his eyes. He could see a brilliantly
decorated ballroom, and five couples united and ready
to face anything together, even a cynical Flint Falcon.

Flint closed his eyes and saw the image he wanted to
see above all others: Leslie, laughing as she sent a
sideways look at him from her long, green eyes. Leslie, curling her arms around him to draw him into the
silken warmth of her body. Leslie, raising her chin and
refusing to cry when he stepped away from the bed to
leave her. Leslie.

He had dreaded leaving, afraid she'd weep and
plead with him to stay. Flint had dreaded it because
he'd been afraid of what seeing her cry, hearing her
plead, would do to him. But Leslie had not wept, she
hadn't pleaded. She had released him, her smile confident with belief in his promise to call her. Leslie had
not shut the door on the silken cage, she had opened
it.

Lifting his head, Flint stared for long seconds at his
vision of freedom. Then, decisively, he turned his back
to it to stride purposefully to his desk. Reaching for
the phone, he punched in a long-distance number. His
gaze drifted to the small desk clock as he heard the
first ring. The slim second hand was making the up-
ward sweep from the nine.

"Hello?" Leslie said at the instant the second hand aligned with the other two hands on the clock.

"Happy New Year, darling. I love you." Flint's voice was low but resolute. "Will you marry me?"

"For after all, in the end, isn't love the only thing that matters?"

There was an instant of quivering silence, and then a growing swell of applause and shouts of approval as the audience rose to their feet.

Standing in the middle of the uproar, Flint stared up at the stage as the actress receiving the acclaim sank into a graceful bow. Watching her take bow after bow, Flint felt a warmth of pride spread throughout his body. Leslie's performance had been nothing less than magnificent. Flint's eyes filled and he blinked to clear his vision, coolly unconcerned with whomever might witness tears rolling down his sharply sculpted face. He stood thus through eight curtain calls and continued to stand while the enthusiastic patrons slowly left the theater. When all but a few stragglers were gone, he made his way backstage.

Flint didn't approach the dressing room, which was surrounded by laughing, chattering people. Instead, he strolled to the stage door to pass the time in conversation with the guard. Propped indolently against the wall, Flint went unnoticed by the departing well-wishers, except for several interested glances from bright feminine eyes.

Flint waited a long time, but when the star finally left her dressing room, she walked directly to him.

"Was I all right?" Leslie asked coyly, gazing up at him and fluttering her eyelashes. The guard chuckled. Flint frowned.

"Just for being cute," he said coolly, drawing her arm through his, "I'm going to make you wait until we get home to hear my opinion." Calling a good-night to the guard, he hustled her out the door and into the waiting limo.

"You're a bully," Leslie informed him, smoothing her hair with one hand. "And a sorehead, too."

"Sailing on an adrenaline high, are you?" Flint inquired politely.

"Yes." Leslie stroked her hand down from her hair to the mink coat draped across her shoulders. "And I want to party."

Flint laughed softly. "I hate to be trite, but oh, darling, have I got a party for you." He was still smiling suggestively when the limo glided to the curb in front of a posh uptown address. "Out, woman," he ordered as the driver pulled the door open. "I'm anxious to get this party started."

In true star fashion, Leslie swept from the car, across the sidewalk and into the elegantly decorated lobby of the large building. Catching Flint around the waist with one arm and grasping his hand, Leslie waltzed Flint to the elevator and, ever the gentleman, Flint obliged. In the elevator, she made do with holding his hands and swaying back and forth. She literally danced along the wide corridor to their apartment door.

"I'm going to have to think of something to gentle you down from cloud nine," Flint observed, following her rhythmically moving body into the ornate foyer. Leslie tangoed into the white-carpeted living room, then spun to face him.

"I've been known to gentle very quickly from a sizzling kiss," she purred provocatively.

"From whom?" Arching one eyebrow, Flint walked slowly toward her. As he closed in on her, her expression altered from euphoria to uncertainty.

"Did you really enjoy my performance, Flint?"

"What's this?" Sliding his arms around her, Flint drew her into a loose embrace. "You were radiant, glorious," he said with frank admiration and honesty. "And you don't need to hear me say it to know it's true."

"You're wrong, Flint." Unmindful of the mink, which had slipped from her shoulders to the floor, Leslie gazed up at him with her love glowing from her eyes. "You are the only one I need to hear it from. I like to hear it from the others," she admitted with a smile, "but I need to hear it from you."

"Okay, I'll tell you." Flint gazed intently into her eyes. "While I stood there with the rest of that clamoring audience, tears of pride ran down my face."

Leslie's eyes widened with shock as she absorbed the magnitude of her husband's confession. Flint Falcon had wept! The mere concept staggered her. She had caused tears to fall from her Falcon's eyes! Incredible!

"Flint?" Leslie couldn't quite decide if she was thrilled or terrified.

"You were that good, darling, and I love you until it hurts." A slow smile slanted his lips. "But I want to know who in hell has been giving you sizzling kisses?"

Bubbling again, Leslie glanced at him. "Well, you see, there's this deliciously sexy gambler from Atlantic City and—Flint!" she squealed, laughing as he swung her into his arms and made for the bedroom with long strides.

"Deliciously sexy, umm?" Flint murmured as he undressed her with haste.

"Oh, yes," Leslie sighed, performing the same service for him.

"And does this gambler lay claim to other attributes?" he inquired, easing her onto the bed and under him.

"Many," Leslie whispered, stroking her palm over his warm skin. "But the most important is, he can lay claim to me."

"And he will."

And he did.

*   *   *   *   *

*Get reacquainted with characters featured in
Joan Hohl's trilogy for Desire in
FOREVER SPRING—Paul Vanzant and
Karen Mitchell's story. Don't miss it—
available in March from
Silhouette Special Edition!*

The passionate saga
that began with SARAH continues in the compelling,
unforgettable story of

Elizabeth

MAURA SEGER

In the aftermath of the Civil War, a divided nation—and two tempestuous hearts—struggle to become one.